Down to the
SUMMIT

Down to the SUMMIT

JOAN SLATALLA

authorHOUSE®

AuthorHouse™ LLC
1663 Liberty Drive
Bloomington, IN 47403
www.authorhouse.com
Phone: 1-800-839-8640

Published by AuthorHouse   07/11/2013

ISBN: 978-1-4817-7337-9 (sc)
ISBN: 978-1-4817-7335-5 (hc)
ISBN: 978-1-4817-7336-2 (e)

Library of Congress Control Number: 2013911783

PREFACE

I do not know if the ceremonies performed by the Hopi are necessary to maintain the balance of the universe. I do know that the Hopi people believe this to be true. Religion to the Hopi is extremely private and personal. Only those initiated into one of their religious societies are privy to knowledge of the ceremonies performed by that society.

According to Mr. Leigh Jenkins, one time Cultural Preservation Director for the Hopi tribe, it is not necessary that the outside world understand the Hopi ceremonies. It is enough that everyone receives the benefits which befall all life on earth when these ceremonies are performed. To Mr. Jenkins, the world inhabited by the Hopi is paradise, and their job is to maintain that paradise.

I have never been initiated into any Hopi religious society, and have no first-hand knowledge of the Hopi ceremonies. Only as an observer have I been fortunate enough to feel the power of the participant's communion with the ancient rhythms and prayers of their ancestors. I've read extensively materials pertaining to the Hopi; which Mr. Jenkins would not endorse as accurate. On that note, I wish the reader to be aware that any accounts of ceremonies in this story are purely fictional. They are meant to reflect the sacred nature of the rites performed by Native Americans. They are not intended to replicate a true ceremony.

I am grateful that nearly ten-thousand people who make up the Hopi Tribe still devote their existence to cosmic harmony. Finally, out of respect for Mr. Jenkins and the Hopi Tribe, I wish to explain the term Anasazi. While I have occasionally used that word in reference to their ancestors due to its popular use in modern American culture, I want the reader to know that these ancients are known to the Hopi as Hisatsinom (Hee-sut-see-nom) meaning people of long ago. Anasazi is a Navaho word which can translate in English to ancient one or ancient enemy. Thus the term Anasazi can be considered by the Hopi as a derogatory term as the Hopi way is a way of peace.

CHAPTER I

Shaman

Shaman stared into the distance and remembered his grandfather's words.

"Don't let the night steal your sight."

The evening's moisture-laden air teased him with the rare promise of rainfall. His skin, accustomed to the dry Arizona climate, tingled in anticipation.

Shaman imagined the scents of cactus and mesquite and the swaying of palm leaves. The phantom leaves conjured visions of an impending storm, and for a moment he was a young graduate student in 2010 making his way to the university library. Soon the remembered smells evaporated, and the missing palm leaves fell silent. Dr. Shaman Thomas, senior anthropology professor at the University of Arizona, turned his collar up against the promise of a drizzle that would go unfulfilled.

A sense of déjà vu robbed him of the pleasant mood he had felt only a moment ago. He rubbed his arms to ward off a sudden chill and hurried into the library, nodding to the few young faces in the common room. The students nodded back. One—who looked like he might actually spring to attention—nearly raised his hand to salute. Shaman quickly tapped a forefinger to his brow, dislodging a silvered wave of copper hair.

Behind the granite counter, the librarian's face was averted, half hidden behind her long, dark hair. For a moment Shaman expected to see Rachel, turquoise eyes flashing, turn and offer her help gathering the references he wanted. When this librarian turned, his momentary excitement vanished. He looked into the questioning, sable eyes of a near-child and snapped back to reality. Twice in the last few minutes he had stepped back in time nearly forty years.

"Can I help you, Dr. Thomas? Is something wrong?"

"No, I was just remembering something from a long time ago. I called ahead for some North American Indian references. Are they ready?" The professor said looking disconcerted.

"Yes, they're right here. Do you need help carrying them?"

"I can manage, thank you." Being surrounded by all this youth could drain a man's psyche. Shaman remembered when he, too, had thought any person over 50 was ancient.

Surely I don't look so decrepit I can't carry a few books! By the time he passed through the main lobby, each book felt like it was bound in stone.

Pride goeth before a fall you damn fool. I should have taken her up on that offer. But at sixty-three, Shaman had no intentions of giving in to feeling old just because he had outlived eighty-five percent of the population. He shifted the weight and exited through a side door to a flight of stone steps leading to a large underground chamber.

The feeling of déjà vu grew stronger. Shaman peered down the dimly lit stairs. Two white-shrouded specters approached from the bowels of the library. Shaman hesitated until the med-students said in unison, "Good evening, Dr. Thomas."

What was I expecting, apparitions? Shaman laughed aloud at his momentary anxiety. The weight of the books and his own momentum hurried Shaman along as he spoke briefly to the white-clad students. With his backside, he hit the release bar on the thick, metal door and headed for the quietest recesses of the stacks.

He wiped the perspiration from his face and dropped his books on the old wooden desk that was tucked in behind stacks of documents few people ever sought. His own thesis on the mythical sipapu hole probably now rested here, yellowing with age amid the massive collection of paper.

Shaman glanced at the files. He wished that he could be as sure now as he had been when he wrote that thesis that the sipapu hole was more than a myth, and it was only a matter of time until he found it.

It's 2048. My time is running out. He gave the chain on the antiquated lamp a gentle tug, and a warm glow highlighted the top of the old, scarred maple desk. He folded his lanky frame into the long-cherished captain's chair and opened the first reference book.

The overhead light went out, and Shaman heard the exit door slam. In the maze of books and files the beam from his reading lamp was all that competed with the blackness of the echoing repository. For a long while only the faint scratch of his pen could be heard.

Suddenly, a voice broke the silence.

"Is that you, Dr. Thomas?"

Shaman jumped halfway out of his chair. Between palpitations, he recognized his visitor. It was Charles Reed, one of the post-docs. For a Hopi, Charlie really stood out. About the only physical character Charlie had in common with his race was his short stature. In contrast to a typical Hopi's jet-black hair and eyes almost as dark, Charlie's were nearly colorless, as was his skin.

"Charlie, are you trying to give me a heart attack? I didn't think anyone else was down here."

"Sorry," Shaman's visitor apologized. Charlie perched one hip on the corner of Shaman's desk and glanced over his shoulder into the surrounding blackness.

"I wouldn't recommend that heart attack down here, professor." Charlie glanced at the pile of research material. "What project has you working so hard?"

Shaman closed the latest tome, replacing it with another from the stack of reference works.

"My granddaughter arrives tomorrow. I'm looking for new territory to explore on our annual trek to hunt for the legendary opening to the Underworld. You're working pretty late yourself."

"Not for me." Charlie ran a hand through his flaxen hair. "Hell, I spend so much time down here I didn't know my girlfriend had left me 'til I got a letter from her."

Shaman remembered his own late nights in this same library. Of course, at the time, he had been a little older than Charlie was now.

The thought of his over-four-decade majority made Shaman sit up a little straighter and square his broad shoulders. Now that his heart had stopped pounding, he relaxed in the little circle of warm light that held the surrounding shadows at bay. He could hear insects scurrying among the day's refuse lying about in the shadows.

"Hard work always pays off in the end, Charlie. But you mustn't neglect the people you care about."

Charlie ignored the light-hearted reprimand. He liked Professor Thomas because Shaman was always willing to extend himself to share his invaluable experiences with any student who showed an interest. Charlie cleared his throat and unconsciously lowered his voice, as though a more manly voice was required to ask the revered professor a personal question.

"Speaking of names, Dr. Thomas, how did you end up with Shaman? It's not your run-of-the-mill nom de plume."

Shaman pushed his work aside to enjoy a few moments of conversation with the inquisitive little albino.

"It was my mom's idea. One of her ancestors was the daughter of a Pueblo priest and something of a healer. Dad was holding out for Sean, but he had to settle for Sham as a nickname. Mom thought the name might help me develop an interest in Native Americans or at least in medicine."

"My son the shaman," Charlie chuckled. "Looks like she was right, Dr. Thomas. With that red hair and blue eyes, Indian wouldn't be my first guess, but everyone knows you're the expert on them. I guess we have your mom to thank for that."

Charlie glanced at his watch. The professor probably wanted to return to his research, but the darkness enveloping everything beyond their small area added a sense of intimacy that invited conversation like some elitist men's club. Of course, Charlie would have his own chair at a club; one where his feet could touch the floor.

"I met a friend of yours, Clyde White Antelope, over at Chaco Canyon last week," Charlie said from his desk perch. "Now, he looks the part; with that jet-black hair and copper complexion. Him, I can picture with a feather or two. He mentioned that you guys used to stick together like glue. He's in jurisprudence, right?"

"It's a good thing you chose pathology and not diplomacy, Charlie. Nobody will ever accuse you of being politically correct. You're right, though, he looks as Native American as his name. He's Navaho and Hopi. Clyde White Antelope finally came unglued and went off to be a lawyer in Albuquerque."

Charlie shifted his weight, careful not to disrupt Shaman's notes. Now neither foot could reach the floor, but at least his butt wouldn't be numb on one side.

"The way the Navaho and Hopi are always battling over land, Clyde must have had to do some high stepping to wade through the middle of that feud."

"Still, you know they do sometimes intermarry," Sham answered. "Besides, Clyde's mom made the best fry bread in the country. It was as light as snow on your tongue; tasted like a doughnut without the sugar and nothing but air inside. A man would be a fool to pass up a woman who can cook like that just because of a few hundred years of tribal rivalry." Sham's mouth watered as he remembered the taste.

"It must have been fat-free, too," Charlie interrupted Sham's mental feast with a compliment to Sham's still muscular physique.

"I guess Clyde and I ran it off. His family lived on our ranch. We were raised like brothers." Sham held his hand to the light to display a jagged scar from the base of the thumb into the palm. "We even drew blood to make it official."

Charlie's stomach churned as he peered at the ritual scar.

"From the looks of that, you had some second thoughts."

"It wouldn't have been my choice," Shaman admitted. "But Clyde was always big on ritual. Sometimes I think that's what I miss the most; his inflexible belief in the necessity of ritual." Shaman gazed into the darkness as though it might still hold a trace of the presence of his old friend.

"When he finally opted for law school, I probably should have followed suit—no pun intended. I certainly knew that anthropology wouldn't pay as well as law."

Charlie shifted his weight to his wrists and propelled himself to the floor. He turned and looked directly into Sham's eyes. The room grew even quieter, and Shaman found himself holding his breath as Charlie spoke.

"Shaman, your discoveries are more important than money. Surely, you know that. It's always about history."

Shaman stared at Charlie. The cherub face with pale eyes was Charlie's, but the remark was strangely out of character, and it was the first time the tiny pathologist had ever called him by his first name.

Before Sham could utter a reply, Charlie blinked, as though waking from a nap, and started for the exit.

"Well, Dr. Thomas, I'm beginning to feel like a ghoul, only leaving these stacks in the dark of night, and all this talk of fry bread has wakened the old garbage pit. It's time for a little nocturnal munching. Don't work too hard."

Shaman watched a more recognizable Charlie, ever the clown, move toward the exit with an exaggerated limp, dragging one foot and holding his cheek to his shoulder, Igor-style.

"It'll save me a trip if you hit that switch on your way out," Shaman called to Charlie's form melting into the shadows only a few feet away. He heard the exit door open and close as Charlie left without acknowledging his request, and Shaman was once again alone in his tiny circle of light.

What a strange little man. He was right about one thing: Clyde is the real Indian, the one who should be huddled over these books in this underground dwelling.

Now the dark room seemed too empty, too silent. He tried to return to his books, but his mind drifted to pleasant memories of experiences shared with his childhood friend. As his notes became doodles, his research became daydreams of young men tracking wild animals through ancient ruins.

Suddenly Shaman sat up straight. What had happened to the light? He was cold, and the cavernous room was as dark as the inside of his pocket. I'm underground. I've been buried alive!

"Stop it, you ninny. You've been asleep in the library. The light must have burned out," Sham scolded himself aloud and found some comfort in the sound of his own voice.

He fumbled for the lamp and pulled the chain, but the blackness was not broken. He groped for the material on the desk, shoveled his notes into his briefcase and felt for the dark stacks that would guide him toward the stairs.

"You are needed," a barely intelligible whisper brushed his ear as he reached the door. Shaman flicked the light switch with no effect.

"Charlie, is that you?" Sham called toward the echoing void, "Did you forget something?" Silence, he was beginning to feel like Jonah—swallowed by a library. He entered the dark stairwell and started quickly up the stone steps. A strong hand clamped on his wrist, stopping him in mid-stride.

"You are needed." A voice, louder now, came not from the vicinity of the hand, but from somewhere else, like an echo bouncing off canyon walls after someone screamed. Sham recognized the voice that had wakened him with those same words many years ago. He jerked around expecting to confront a prankster, but no one was there.

He ran the rest of the way to the empty lobby and made his way past the granite counter. A security guard stood at the tall double doors. Shaman had only once before seen a guard in the library. Just as on that previous occasion, this one was a dead-ringer for his own father.

"You are needed," the guard whispered as Shaman raced outside. He turned, but the doors were bolted behind him. Debris scurrying across his path triggered a memory of dried leaves rustling past his feet when he had been ushered from the library in 2010.

As though it was happening now, he recalled how he had raced to his one-room apartment, turned on the light to chase away the shadows and grabbed a cold beer from the pint-sized refrigerator which rested at the foot of his bed. Unexplainably, he had picked up the phone and dialed his parents, only to find a Detective Osinski on the other end.

"I've been trying to reach you," the detective said as gently as possible, but the words reached Shaman's ear like a shout. "I'm afraid your parents have been shot!"

Sham saw himself running through the glass entrance to the antiseptic lobby at the county hospital near his parents' ranch.

Detective Osinski, whose wandering eye and rumpled coat made him look like a bad imitation of Columbo, was there to greet him. "I'm sorry, son, your mom is in ICU. Your dad didn't make it."

After all these years, the wound caused by those words was still raw. His legs lost the ability to support him. Shaman leaned against the library entrance, grabbed the doorknob for support and, once again, experienced the jolt of that revelation.

While Shaman clung to the door, his mind continued to replay that awful day. His protesting limbs moved him shakily toward the elevator that inched its way up to the intensive care unit. A crisp young nurse, tagged Ms. Warden, escorted him down a sterile hall. He heard again the discordant beat of the life-support machines hissing, clicking, and beeping a death-watch symphony behind the door of each cubicle they passed.

In his mother's room, he heard the quiet whoosh as fluids were suctioned from her body and the accompanying beep of the IV monitor as they were replaced. The nurse tended to the myriad tubes snaking out from beneath the blankets.

"Deborah Thomas" was written in bright orange on the identification card attached to the bed. She looked so tiny and frail. He smelled the rainwater scent that had enfolded him when he buried his face in her hair. Her eyes fluttered, and she murmured,

"Thank God you've come. I've been calling for you. I need to tell you something. The water . . . the unfinished sentence drifted away as he put a straw to her lips. A moment later she spoke of his first day of school.

"Remember how frightened you were, Shaman? You held my hand so tightly, but by the time we reached the door, you insisted on going in alone. You were always an independent child. I know you're going to be fine, dear. I have to go to your father now."

"No Mom, don't go!"

On the library steps, Shaman relived the emptiness he had felt as her hand fell away. He wiped the tears from his eyes. He must get home to Rachel.

Please God let Rachel be all right.

Chapter II

Rachel

A third cup of coffee only added to Rachel's anxiety. She rinsed the mug, went to her bedroom, pulled on a baggy sweater over her T-shirt and shorts, before changing the shorts for a pair of faded jeans and sat at her dressing table. Her slender fingers quickly braided the still dark tresses. Sham should have been here hours ago.

"He probably fell asleep in the library," Rachel assured her worried face in the mirror. The face tried to look relieved by this bit of information but couldn't quite pull it off. The turquoise eyes did brighten momentarily, dispelling the threatening dark circles beneath them.

Anxiety made one last stab at holding her attention. *The roads are in terrible condition. Heavy clouds are moving in from the south. Even if they don't bring rain, they could push the pollution index off the charts. What if his jeep broke down or the air filtration system clogged?*

"Don't be such a worry-wart," she admonished the still-attractive-but-aging face. "Shaman can take care of himself."

Rachel moved to a little paneled alcove off the great room and sat at her computer. Staring past the monitor, she peered through the window, imagining a family of quail—a cautious, feathered drum major leading a string of chicks, each hardly larger than a half-dollar, while the mother served as rear guard. I miss the animals scurrying about their business. I can't remember the last time I heard a coyote howl or a donkey bray.

For the next hour she tried to describe some of the vibrant colors that had filled her life before the world became a great gray place devoid of most animal life; over the years, one ecological system after another succumbing to pollution, weather changes and disease.

At last, happy with the results of her efforts, she considered making another pot of coffee, rejected that idea, and went instead to the library.

The warm, natural woods and brightly colored rugs soothed her. Rachel was increasingly more content to research the lessons of the past from the comfort of her easy chair and leave the strenuous pursuit of archaeological digs to younger explorers. She retrieved a history of the Hopi clans from the large, walnut bookcase and curled into her fetal reading position.

She perused Edmund Nequatewa's rendition of how the Water Clan Society came to Walpi and demonstrated their power to bring rain. Soon, the stirring tale of heavy snows and cloudbursts went unheeded as memories flooded in of another ritual, the Ya Ya, where human and animal spirits meld.

In Chaco Canyon, Clyde had sworn Sham and Rachel to secrecy, and neither ever mentioned to another living soul that they had observed the rarely performed Hopi ritual. She relived the memory.

Dancers, clad in animal skins, stamped a hypnotic beat on the hard-packed ceremonial floor as the fire they encircled grew in intensity, and the air around them took on a life with a resounding heartbeat.

A coyote-clad dancer uttered a pure animal howl and seemed to appear and disappear before their eyes. An antelope-clad figure—or was he a real antelope?—leaped high above the fire, while the crackling flames provided a backdrop of millions of red fireflies winging their way to the stars.

Some dancers seemed to leap, or fly, to the branches on surrounding trees. Another glance and only crows were visible on those same branches. Seconds later, a dancer wearing a feathered headdress swooped within inches of their faces, startling them with a shrieking Caw! Caw! Rachel knew that they had witnessed something far beyond the usual ceremony that marks the changing of the seasons. The memory brought a shiver even now.

Rachel's reverie was interrupted by the crunch of tires on the gravel drive. The grinding gears of an antique truck announced that it would not be Shaman. Pappy Coyote had gone to fetch Zoe in the only automobile he was willing to drive. Every time the rusting heap sputtered to life, Rachel was amazed. Not only had the engine been rebuilt several times with rapidly dwindling spare parts, but Pappy had to produce homemade gasoline to fuel it.

She rushed to the porch to greet the wrinkled old Indian and her granddaughter. Pappy moved quickly for his age; although no one knew for sure just how old he was. His dark hair swung free beneath the bandana tied around his forehead as he mounted the porch with the heavy baggage.

Rachel hugged her granddaughter tightly and held her at arm's length.

"You look more like your mother every day, Zoe."

The just-turned-teenager's eyes flashed her happiness at this compliment. She had grown two whole inches in the past six months, and her face had thinned down a bit as the baby fat gave way to a more mature bone structure. She, too, had noticed her resemblance to the picture of her mother, which was always with her.

While Rachel and Zoe exchanged hugs, Pappy leaned against the porch railing and looked toward the distant hills.

"Would you like to take time to have tea?" Rachel invited.

The old Indian turned toward Rachel and hoisted Zoe's trunk onto his shoulder.

"Guess I'd better just get this stuff in the house and head back out. The gasoline distiller needs some attention, unless you need me for something else." Pappy moved toward the door. Rachel spoke to his back.

"You know, Pappy, if we replace that dinosaur with an electric truck, you won't have to worry about making gasoline." Pappy paused halfway through the doorway.

"No cause to be doing that," he mumbled. "It ain't much trouble to make a little gas." Then he carried the luggage into the house. "Good to have you back Miss Zoe," thrown over his shoulder as an afterthought. The screen-door slammed lightly behind him.

"Is something wrong with Pappy, Grandma?" Zoe asked.

Rachel was surprised by the question. "He doesn't look ill," she thought aloud. "You saw how easily he handled that trunk, and it's nearly as big as he is. Why? Did something happen on the way home?"

What else might she find to worry about? *First Shaman falls asleep in the library (surely that's what happened). Maybe I should try to reach him at the university. But Sham hates it when I coddle him too much; says it makes him feel like a dithering old fool. This is definitely not a good time for something to be wrong with Pappy.* Zoe noticed the strain in Rachel's voice and tried to take the words back.

"I didn't mean to upset you. It's probably all in my imagination." She ignored the big rocking chair and leaned against the railing that Pappy had just vacated.

"He's never been a big talker, but he's usually interested in what I've been doing. Today, I might as well have been talking to myself when I told him about my trip to Canyon de Chelly. (Canyon de Shay) Maybe he's getting hard of hearing."

In the perpetual dusk, Rachel propped herself next to Zoe; two women, one at the beginning, the other near the end of her years of nurturing and worrying about those whom they love.

"Well, we'll keep an eye on him. I don't know what we'd do if anything happened to Pappy. He's been here longer than I have."

Zoe took in the view of the rambling old cedar building and sighed. She squeezed Rachel's still trim waist, glad that her grandmother looked so well.

"It's good to be home," she said with meaning.

Zoe loves this place as much as I do. Rachel, too, let her eye roam over the much loved ranch, and her mind drifted to her own arrival as Shaman's wife. Her nose twitched from the remembered smell of sun-drenched orange and lemon orchards that graced the ranch before succumbing to the heavy pollution. She had quickly become attached to the roadrunners nested in those trees; even though she hated it when one of the ungainly birds streaked by with baby quail feet dangling from its beak, the poor baby quail peeping frantically.

Had she wasted less sympathy when the victim was a snake dangling across a roadrunner's beak?

"Grandma, Zoe tightened her grip on her grandmother's waist, urging her toward the door.

"Sorry, dear, I was just reminiscing."

"Where is Grandpa?"

"He should be here any minute." Rachel said. "He's been researching new terrain for the two of you to explore."

"We're going to find it this year," Zoe replied confidently. She settled comfortably in her favorite chair by the big bay window. "So what have you been up to lately?"

"I wrote a new poem. And, oh! I began documenting a kiva last week." Rachel settled down in the easy chair across from Zoe and watched as the news of a new kiva—like handing a treasure map to an old prospector—brought a sparkle to Zoe's eyes. The same glow lit Zoe's face whenever she entered one of these underground ceremonial rooms and rushed to the center to look for the symbolic sipapu hole, hoping that this time it would be the real staircase to the Underworld.

"Where's the kiva? When did you find it?" Zoe asked excitedly

"Actually, it was years ago. Shaman and I were exploring the ruins at Betatakin, but we never got around to documenting it. Recently, the kiva popped into my head, and I felt negligent that I never mapped it."

Zoe was surprised that her grandmother had used the Navajo name for the Hopi place, Kawestima. Today everyone, including Zoe, used the more common Navajo term, but Rachel usually chose to refer to the old ruins by their Hopi names.

"Will I get to see it soon?" Zoe pleaded.

"Not this week, but maybe before you go back to your tutor."

"Can't we go back to home-schooling this year? I'd much rather stay here with you and Grandpa."

Before answering, Rachel added an artificial log to the big stone fireplace, and wondered if she was doing the right thing, sending Zoe to a private tutor. Zoe watched the worry lines appear on Rachel's face and seemed to read her mind.

"Why did you decide on a tutor for me?" Zoe asked.

"I think learning in the company of other young people adds a great deal to the experience. Public schools were fine in my day, but that was a long time ago."

"When did home-schooling become so popular?"

"When the National Work Force Curriculum was foisted on our own children in the guise of education," Rachel answered. "Students (the national workforce, in government doubletalk), spent much of their time interning in whatever fields were most available in their particular geographic area. Before long, a lot of students thought Shakespeare was something you got at a fast food restaurant."

"That might not be all bad." Zoe made a face. Clearly, Shakespeare was not one of her favorite subjects.

"Many graduated barely literate enough to find their way to that workplace. Fewer and fewer went on to University." Rachel recalled the mindless disinterest that her little personal campaign against "school-to-work" had aroused.

"Oh, our tutor informed us that next year may be his last," Zoe said a little too gleefully. "Will I be staying at home if the residence closes?" she asked hopefully.

"We'll certainly discuss it with your grandfather." Maybe Zoe should spend more time with us now. She'll be ready for university in another year. Shaman would love to have her with us all the time, and so would I. If he isn't here in half an hour, I'm definitely calling the university, and then the police. Anything could happen on that road.

※　　※　　※

Shaman sped along as fast as the potholes would allow. Hell of a time for a transmission black-out. I can't even call. His recent experience in the library had filled him with anxiety. He couldn't shake the feeling that something terrible awaited him. Would he find Rachel and Zoe alive and well? He tried for a little more speed and nearly lost control when he had to dodge a large area that had broken away from the road.

"In the meantime, can I see your new poem?" Zoe interrupted Rachel's thoughts. Rachel produced her latest work before going behind the floral-tiled counter where all the missing plants that Rachel loved so much were forever depicted under a bright glaze across the counter-top separating the living and kitchen areas. While the tea steeped, Rachel studied Zoe draped across a chair, her shapely young legs dangling over one chair arm, back resting against the other. The so-familiar child's body now had the contours of a young lady, and the ever-present French braid had been traded for a fashionable shoulder-length cut.

She's growing so fast, she'll have to think about starting a family soon. I wish she had more time. Whatever possessed us to allow hazardous waste dumps next to our water supply and nuclear reactors damn near on top of fault lines? She thought.

The day was getting as dark as Rachel's thoughts, and still no sign of Shaman, but Zoe hadn't picked up on Rachel's anxiety as she gave her grandmother's poem the attention it deserved.

ARIZONA ALCHEMY

Nature's magic color game
Is awesome to behold
As sunset streaks across the sky
Changing stone to yellow gold
And setting snow white clouds aflame
While nature's sorcerer does play
Creating colors unrefined
A molten lava flow
Erodes the edge of time
Transmuting night from yesterday
Changed once more to blackest ore
Night's nocturnal ambiance
Assures a muted rest
To refresh the alchemist
Before the day must be restored
Play then turns to honest toil
For light must soon abide
In brilliant shades of energy
To feed the needs of ocean tides
And urge new life to sun-drenched soil

Zoe was moved. She could feel the power and the beauty of a sunset she had never experienced as it enacted the changing of the guard. She could see the light burning away on the horizon, leaving darkness not yet studded with jewels, and felt the mounting anticipation of the newness of tomorrow.

"I love this poem, Grandma," Zoe proclaimed. Rachel barely had time to acknowledge this seal of approval before Zoe turned the conversation back to her main interest.

"Tell me more about this new Kiva. Is it large? Can you tell which society used it? Does it have a fire pit?" Her questions came rapid-fire.

"Slow down. Yes, maybe, and yes." Rachel laughed at Zoe's excitement and set their tea on a table between them.

"I'll tell you all the details, but first I want to hear about what you've been learning."

Zoe laid the poem aside and smothered her excitement about the new kiva. It didn't take long to warm to the subject of her latest school project.

"I just finished a report on the ancient cave dwellings of the Anasazi . . ."

"Did you remember that they were known to the Hopi as Hisatsinom (Hee-sut'-see-nom) . . ."

"And that Anasazi is a Navaho term which has become more popular. Yes, Grandma, and I knew you would ask."

"Okay, I'll start lunch, and I won't interrupt anymore," Rachel said as she returned to the kitchen with her tea.

"I included the intaglios, those huge land drawings that only make sense from the air, (this to ensure that her grandmother knew she understood what she was writing about), and I mentioned the Fremont petroglyphs in Utah where some of the subjects could be astronauts wearing bubble helmets. "Mostly I concentrated on how the Anasazi, the Hisatsinom, disappeared mysteriously nearly a thousand years ago. Isn't it eerie, all those people just vanishing like that?

Rachel was more concerned with the vanished Shaman. She checked the time again and set the crock of dough aside.

"I know one Navaho who thinks they left in UFOs. How's that for modern thinking? It would explain your astronauts, too." Rachel hid her own concerns about Shaman's late return behind light conversation and the rattle of pans in her kitchen.

"What else did you write about?"

"I wrote a lot about the ruins in Canyon de Chelly."

Known to the Hopi as Koyongtupqa, Rachel thought, but did not interrupt. Zoe sipped at her tea before continuing.

"I loved the 'White House'. It was like a big pearl set above the topaz ruins below. The winds whispering through the empty rooms sounded like voices chanting a rain ritual."

"Let's hope they did it right. One little mistake, and it might not rain for seventy years," Rachel quipped.

"Oh, Grandma, seriously, do you think it was really the long drought that caused them to pack up and leave forever?"

The crunch of gravel covered Rachel's sigh of relief as Shaman finally arrived. Zoe greeted him with a bear hug; the Anasazi, for the moment, forgotten. Sham threw Rachel a kiss and returned Zoe's hug. Rachel thought he looked troubled, or was she just projecting her own feelings. Shaman smiled, and Rachel felt better.

"You're getting so big, Zoe. You're nearly up to my shoulder already. How old were you on your last birthday, twenty-four?"

"You know I turned thirteen last month, Grandpa." Zoe laughed and held up her hand to display his birthday gift.

"I love the turquoise ring, and (so Rachel wouldn't feel slighted) the pot Grandma sent is the best piece in my collection." Shaman moved to the counter and gave Rachel a peck on the cheek.

"Sorry, I fell asleep," his only explanation for his late arrival. Rachel patiently set a cup of steaming tea in front of him. "You're like my mother, Zoe," Shaman said between quick sips. "Pretty soon you'll have pots all over the house. As a kid, I could hardly turn around for fear of breaking some irreplaceable piece of pottery. I was forever tripping over that Two-Gray-Hills rug in her bedroom. I'd have to grab the four-poster to keep from crashing into her favorites at the foot of the bed."

Zoe heard the wistful note in Shaman's words and knew he was thinking of his parents. She picked up her own cup and joined him at the counter.

"I still can't imagine why anyone would kill your parents and then break all the pots in their house."

"The police finally just wrote it off to someone crazy on dope, or just plain crazy. Maybe I should have done more on my own." Shaman's big shoulders drooped as though an old weight had returned.

"You were in shock, Shaman," Rachel said, trying to salve his guilt.

"Maybe," Shaman agreed, but deep inside all the old self-doubt began to reawaken. "Let's not talk about that now. I want to hear what you've been up to, Zoe. Are you ready for adventure?"

Rachel caught Shaman's sidelong gaze. Something was wrong; something he didn't want to discuss in front of Zoe. They continued to make light conversation while Rachel prepared Kolatquvi, thumbprint bread. She shaped the dough into balls and set them on the counter.

"Remember how I used to call Kolatquvi 'boo bed'?" Zoe asked, automatically making the ritual thumbprint in the middle of each ball before Rachel put them into a colander to cook over boiling water. The memory made Rachel smile.

"You loved to watch the ash tint the cornmeal blue. I think your mother had to make boo bed at every meal for the next year."

The rest of the day was a time of catching up. After Zoe retired, a lively fire danced in the large stone fireplace. The artificial blaze aspired to being as good as one that would once have been produced by huge cedar logs. With the aid of modern chemistry, even the cedar aroma had been added. On the worn leather sofa, Rachel cuddled warm and cozy against Sham's hip.

"Sweetheart, do you remember what I told you about the night my folks were murdered?" Sham whispered with his lips buried in her hair. Rachel knew that it was time to discuss the things left unspoken earlier. She nodded and waited for Shaman to continue.

"Nearly the same thing happened last night. I must have fallen asleep over my research. The next thing I knew, that voice was calling me again. It repeated the same phrase, 'You are needed.' I couldn't get out of there fast enough. The eeriest part was my dad was standing at the door like a security guard. It was exactly the same as the night he was killed. Something is going to happen, Rachel. Maybe I shouldn't take Zoe to the ceremony tomorrow.

"Do you think it's something you can control, Shaman? You've always felt there was a reason why we've out-lived our children and most of our friends. Whatever it is, dear, we'll have to accept it. Your spirits will guide you where you need to go. If they want Zoe to be there we can't change it, but I think I'll go along."

"You're right of course. We shouldn't change anything. If it happens tomorrow, then you weren't supposed to be there. Besides, it could be next week or next month. Let's just go to bed and let tomorrow bring what it will. I need to be close to you tonight."

In the darkened bedroom, they rolled toward one another, two old lovers comfortable with their passion. There was no awkwardness as Shaman stroked Rachel's body, fondling her mature breasts, then past her waist to linger on a shapely hip. Rachel's tongue brushed his lips as she welcomed him with a feathery touch across his nipples. From years of experimentation, they knew what made each thrill to the other's touch, and they slowly built their desire, pacing themselves to each other's needs.

CHAPTER III

Old Oraibi

———— ✦ ————

The sunrise was even dimmer than usual, but Shaman felt like whistling.

"My, you're certainly gay this morning." Rachel's muffled voice fought its way from the downy covers.

"Want to stay home and spread a little of that good cheer right here?"

"You know I'd love to," Shaman said with a contrived leer. "But the Hopi ritual won't wait until I decide to come out of hiding. Whatever is in store for me will materialize whether I'm here or somewhere else."

Displaying more composure than she really felt, Rachel smothered her fears, kissed Sham soundly and headed for the kitchen to make breakfast. The table was already set, and the smell of hot coffee made her nose twitch.

"Zoe! What a nice surprise."

"Grandpa said if we want to see the ceremonial dance in Old Oraibi, we should get an early start."

"Well, you certainly took him at his word. That coffee smells wonderful. I wish I could go with you, but if we plan to eat, I need to get those sun panels working.

"Zoe, you know how secretive the Hopi are about their ceremonies. Remember no cameras or tape recorders or sketch pads," Rachel added.

"I know, Grandma. I wouldn't do anything to insult the Hopi people. I think it's great that they still observe the old ways. If more people were like them, maybe the world wouldn't be in the shape it is."

Rachel gave her granddaughter a quick hug. "I know you wouldn't, dear. It was silly of me to think I had to remind you." Rachel gave Zoe a light swat on the bottom.

"Now let's get breakfast. Shaman will be ready soon. He's as excited as you are."

A short time later, Rachel waved pensively and managed a good-bye smile as Shaman's jeep disappeared down the gravel drive. I should have gone with them. Why did I let him talk me out of it?

They were headed into danger. She could feel it like a dark molasses oozing through her mind.

By mid-morning, Shaman and Zoe had checked in at the one small hotel on the reservation. Here the brush was a little heavier. Even a few patches of bladder pod, its bright yellow flowers a treat for the eyes, were waving bravely to the new arrivals. Shaman wondered if the isolation or ritual practices should be credited for a positive effect on the immediate environment.

"Thought we'd catch a nap before the ceremony," Sham said to the clerk who handed him the room keys. "Would you give me a call in an hour?" The clerk's placid face could have been carved of stone.

"Glad to give you the wake-up, but don't know anything about a ceremony."

Sham wasn't surprised. He shouldn't have mentioned the ceremony, as most rituals are not open to the public, and this stranger had no way of knowing that Shaman was a pueblo descendant (distant as the tie might be).

Shaman drove to the rear of the collection of adobe buildings that shared a common courtyard. There a pitiful patch of sulphur flower and more bladder pod lured the eye like a botanical garden; or a natural pharmacy if you happened to be in need of a childbirth aid or relief for painful eyes or snake bite. He parked the jeep behind their assigned rooms and turned to retrieve their backpacks from the rear seat.

"Grandpa, what is it?" Zoe called out. When he turned, she was offering the remainder of a half-eaten sandwich to a large animal that was peering into the open passenger's window.

Shaman quickly dismissed the thought that an albino wolf had somehow managed to survive by raiding the sheep herds that remained on the reservation. Those herds had better protection than the President, and this animal was much too healthy to be feasting on an occasional rodent and the sparse vegetation available in the barren desert.

"I do believe it's a dog, Zoe. Keep your hands away from it." Then he whistled and called to the animal. "Hey, Girl, come here."

Before Zoe could pull her hand back, the dog quickly accepted the welcome snack, answering Sham's question about the animal's diet.

While keeping an eye on Shaman, the dog backed only a few steps away from the jeep, making way for Zoe to step down. Shaman opened Zoe's door. The animal remained a few feet distant, keeping pace and never taking its eyes off Zoe as it accompanied them to their quarters.

Before going to his adjoining room for a much needed nap, Sham made Zoe promise to stay in her room, lock her door and keep her hands out of the animal's mouth.

He headed toward his own welcoming bed, and saw the dog settle itself comfortably in front of Zoe's door.

"Okay, Charlie," Sham named the dog after the little albino pathologist. "You keep an eye on her." For a few minutes he listened to Zoe's humming on the other side of the wall before fatigue carried him away.

An hour later, much refreshed, they were on their way to Old Oraibi. Two villages seemed totally deserted before they reached a locale that professes to be the oldest continuously inhabited town in North America. There they found the primitive, narrow streets choked with modern automobiles.

Trucks and cars were parked in every vacant space. Sham left his own vehicle in a long line of others parked on the precarious shoulder of the cliff. They walked to the center of the village and found the missing inhabitants crowded around the village plaza. The ceremony had already begun.

Shaman and Zoe climbed a mound of earth and broken stones to reach a rooftop. Shaman's copper locks towered above the shiny black pates of the other spectators. Only Zoe's eyes set her apart from any young Hopi. One little raven-haired, black-eyed toddler fascinated by those turquoise pools, pointed to the pair of strangers while tugging on his mother's skirt. The mother quickly turned the child away as if to protect him from the evil eye. No one else acknowledged their presence.

A line of masked dancers dressed in ceremonial kilts half-filled the plaza beneath them. Punctuating their steps with intermittent chants, the dancers communed with the timeless spirits of the universe. Zoe was entranced by the spectacle and the mesmerizing rhythm of the dance. Shaman felt a stirring in his own body, and his feet ached to stamp out the ancient rhythm.

Suddenly, a group of masked kachina spirits emerged from the hole in the top of an underground kiva. Some of them carried willow branches, but Zoe's attention was captured by a few who were actually holding snakes. She was glad to be standing on a rooftop.

After the kachinas arrived, most of the original dancers left the plaza, leaving only three ash-colored men to deal with these spirits. The crowd shouted and laughed as the kachinas pulled those remaining three into a mud bath and taunted them with the willow whips and snakes.

The kachinas dragged one poor soul through the plaza until his only garment was torn from his body, and he was left lying nude in the sand.

"Why did they do that, Grandpa?"

"Maybe they're trying to rid the poor fellow of malevolent spirits which can result from too much contact with Whites," explained Shaman, who had seen similar rituals performed by many different tribes.

Several women holding towels surrounded the nude man, and he fashioned a short kilt from one of their towels. Soon the kachinas returned to their underground ceremonial room, and the people began to disperse.

"Itse!" (darn it) yelled a man rapidly climbing toward Shaman. "You should have told me you were coming." He clasped Shaman's hand with one of his own and threw the other around Shaman's shoulder.

"This is Yöngösonhoya," Shaman introduced Zoe to a Hopi friend who had spotted them on the roof. "Do you know what his name means in English?"

"It's Little Turtle, isn't it? I'm very pleased to meet you, Yöngösonhoya." Zoe thought the name appropriate, as Little Turtle's neck poked forward from his shoulders, and his eyelids drooped until his eyes looked like little walnut slits protruding beneath raven bangs.

"This accurate young interpreter is Zoe, my granddaughter," Shaman introduced Zoe. "We are doing some exploring. It's good to see you again."

Little Turtle took one of her hands into both of his and welcomed her warmly. They did not discuss the ceremony. Both Shaman and Zoe knew that to ask about its meaning or origin would be an intrusion. It was enough that they had been allowed to observe the sacred rite and be moved by its eloquence.

Sham accepted an invitation to visit at his friend's home, the very house they were standing on. Shaman was a full head taller than the doorway to this traditional stone and mud-daubed dwelling which was almost hidden by the mound of rubble that they had climbed earlier.

The original house was one room with a floor of packed earth. A wooden ladder gave access to several upper-story chambers that had been added to accommodate the growing family. These rooms were as sparsely furnished as the original house, with only a few shelves and chairs and an occasional table. A domed oven was still maintained outside of the residence, and while Shaman and Little Turtle visited, their hostess taught Zoe how to bake piki, wafer-thin bread especially revered by the Hopi.

"We caused a bit of a stir up on your roof, Little Turtle," Shaman said to his host. "A little tyke's mom seemed to think he might have been exposed to the evil eye."

"Don't worry about it, my friend. It's just your red hair. Your granddaughter's eyes are a great counterbalance, though."

After sharing the bread, Shaman smacked his lips in appreciation and reminded Zoe that they should get an early start in the morning.

"You are welcome to stay if you are not needed elsewhere," Little Turtle offered.

The phrase made Shaman a little uneasy. "That may well be the case," he replied to his friend, and thanked him for his hospitality. Zoe hated to see the visit end, but anxious to start tomorrow's trek, quickly said her farewells.

Back at the hotel, they found the faithful dog camped patiently beside Zoe's door, where it remained until morning. Zoe had blue cornmeal hotcakes for breakfast in the hotel dining room, saving her last one to feed to her loyal guard. As they drove away, Zoe waved to the big white dog.

CHAPTER IV

After a short drive and three hours of hiking over rough terrain, Shaman's legs were tired. He paused for a moment, steadying his walking stick against the rubble on the slope.

He couldn't shake a growing feeling that the incident in the library would manifest its meaning sooner rather than later.

"Wait up," he called to Zoe, whose more agile body had carried her quite a distance ahead.

"Look, Grandpa, it's some kind of lizard," she answered from about twenty yards uphill. Holding the reptile by the tail with one hand, she picked her way back through the sparse cacti and scrub brush to show him her prize.

Her lovely hair bounced above her shoulders. The thick dark strands concealed a red flame that would have been beautifully highlighted on a sunlit day. Even with today's gray atmosphere, the fine wisps around her face gave the effect of a rosy halo.

"What kind of lizard is it, Grandpa?" He had no idea what kind of lizard—if that mutated thing even was a lizard—swung from its tail in her hand.

"Honestly, Zoe, I'm not sure. The world has changed too quickly for me to keep up," Shaman answered sadly. *Damn that nuclear accident. What were we thinking? Atomic Gods, that's what we thought we were.*

"Don't be sad, Grandpa. It's not your fault." Zoe returned the lizard to the rocky ground and sat down next to Shaman. He put his arm around her.

"Yes, it is my fault. It's everyone's fault. We were bad stewards of what nature blessed us with, and we've left little for our children to inherit.

"You are needed." Shaman started at the words. He had perceived them clearly, but Zoe showed no sign that she had heard anything. Shaman's breath became labored and he coughed. Zoe looked worriedly at the sky.

"The pollution is really bad today, isn't it? Maybe we should start home." She wished her grandfather would wear the portable oxygen tube that many older people kept handy. Some days the air was so heavy you could weigh it. Even in this relatively uninhabited area, the sky was dismal today.

"I'm all right, Zoe. Don't worry about me. I'm not old enough to be classified as Anasazi."

But she thought he looked like he might need a little longer to rest. "Grandpa, tell me again about the people who used to live on this mountain."

Like an Indian storyteller, Shaman believed there was a right way to tell a story, and it should be recited the same way every time. He began as always.

"They were the Hisatsinom, or so the legend goes, the Old Ones who lived in harmony with the land and the sky and the water. They believed that even the rocks possessed a living spirit."

As Shaman spun his tale, Zoe pictured a bygone world of sanctuaries tucked into caves high on the cliff-face populated by these mysterious little people who had disappeared without a trace.

She noticed a large spider—or something that could have been one—dart quickly beneath a nearby rock, just as Shaman mentioned Spider Grandmother in his tale.

"Spider Grandmother led only those who had learned to live peacefully to live in the sunshine on the surface of the earth. The people emerged through the sipapu hole, climbing shakily from deep below the crusty rocks," Shaman was saying.

Zoe wondered if those first people, upon reaching the shock of daylight, had squinted in confusion at the bright sun. Had they marveled at the blue of a pristine sky? What would her own reaction be to these things that she herself had never experienced?

Her excitement mounting, Zoe interrupted the story. "Grandpa, I really think we're going to find it today." Shaman heard the thrill of anticipation in her voice and did not doubt that she could very well be right.

"Tell me again the story of the kiva," Zoe insisted. She had heard Shaman's lecture on the history of the kiva many times, but she once again listened intently as he resumed his tale.

"When the Hisatsinom started building their houses aboveground, they kept the pit house for ceremonies. A symbolic sipapu hole was placed near the center of these underground rooms. Some people think they used it as the passageway for their souls to return to the Underworld."

Zoe knew the story by heart. She harbored hopes that someday the Creator would again call the Anasazi back to the world. She pictured all the sipapu holes in all the kivas opening up to disgorge the ancient Indians. Shaman looked at the encroaching dark clouds. "Maybe we'd better get going. It's not too far now."

They resumed their climb, picking their way carefully around the sharp pebbles and steadying themselves against the boulders that lined the twisted path.

Shaman wondered if the rocks they leaned on were aware of their touch. Could these same rocks recall those Old Ones who left the story of their passing engraved upon the mountain's epidermis like archaic tattoos?

"Look, Grandpa, there's something up there," Zoe called back before running around a large boulder.

It's probably another lizard. He picked up his pace to see what new prize Zoe had found. But he was wrong: This time it was not a lizard.

Zoe ran ahead, around another rock, and stopped abruptly. A woman dressed in skins was standing a few feet away. The woman spoke so softly that Zoe couldn't hear what she was saying. Beckoning Zoe nearer, she repeated the words.

"I am Alo, your spiritual guide."

Then, as though a magnet was pulling her, Zoe was being dragged toward the woman. The pull became a sucking vacuum! Zoe's feet barely touched the ground as she raced uncontrollably toward a large hole behind the strange woman.

Many times Zoe had been warned about the abandoned mine shafts so prevalent in the Arizona countryside. More than a few hikers had been lost to these yawning pits. She called to warn the stranger before looking for something to grab hold of.

As she glanced over her shoulder, Zoe saw that Shaman had rounded the boulders. He reached out in terror. She thought he called her name, but the wind rushing past her face, pulling her toward that dark, looming hole, drowned out all other sound.

With fear pumping adrenaline into him, Shaman ran toward her. He stumbled among the rocks and tripped just as the gaping orifice swallowed his granddaughter. Hurtling downward, dizzy and frightened, Zoe caught a glimpse of her grandfather charging through the hole that was closing above them like a zipper. Then they fell and fell into absolute blackness.

CHAPTER V

Premonition

Rachel worried as she worked. She should have gone with Shaman and Zoe to the ceremony. She recalled many of these long-remembered rites meant to keep nature in harmony, to bring rain, to heal the sick, or comfort the dying. And again the memory of the Ya Ya overshadowed the rest.

She sat down with a cup of coffee and the newspaper and quickly became engrossed in the gruesome details of a body found decapitated. A shadow fell across the paper and Rachel jumped to her feet.

"I didn't mean to startle you," Pappy apologized from the doorway. "I think your sun panels are working fine. If you don't need me, I have a few chores to do."

"No, that's fine, Pappy, but please have a cup of coffee with me first." Rachel put on her I-need-company face, and Pappy moved farther into the room.

"Have you read this story about the body found near Sedona? They're speculating that a new religious cult has moved to Arizona."

"Maybe it was a two-heart."

"You mean a witch? Do you know any witches, Pappy?"

The old cowhand was sorry he had spoken so quickly. He began to fidget with his neckerchief and stared at the flowering vine border that decorated the stucco walls just beneath the ceiling.

"The two-hearts are everywhere," Pappy finally replied haltingly, eyes now darting left and right, as though one might be in the room at this very moment. "No one knows who might be a witch these days. I've heard that they gather sometimes at Koyongtupqa, but I don't know this for sure."

"But do you know any witches, personally?" Rachel put a cup of coffee in Pappy's wrinkled, mahogany hand and coaxed him to sit at the counter. A warm glow briefly lit the window behind them, as though the sun might actually break through the haze today. Rachel enjoyed the fleeting moment, and Pappy relaxed enough to sip from the steaming cup.

"I had a cousin once, name of Gray Eagle, who had an argument with a neighbor, who my cousin said was a witch. The two-heart had a big yellow dog that liked to chase snakes. The dog would sometimes bring them to my cousin's front door and leave them. Gray Eagle built a fence to keep the dog from bringing the snakes to his door. When the two-heart saw the fence, he was very angry. He told Gray Eagle he would be sorry, and my cousin was sure the two-heart had used the evil eye. A week later, Gray Eagle was found dead on his own doorstep."

The brief glimpse of sunshine was a forgotten memory. Rachel looked out at a thickening sky and asked, "Do you really believe that he died because of the evil eye?"

"They did an autopsy at the hospital. They didn't know what he had died from. There were no marks on his body, but there was an awful grimace of pain on his face." Rachel was almost afraid to ask. "What did they find?"

"I wasn't there, but another cousin told me that when the doctor opened Gray Eagle's stomach, it was full of little snakes."

"That's quite a story, Pappy." Rachel's previous apprehension returned tenfold. That must have been one surprised coroner. As Rachel contemplated the coroner's horror upon surgically incising an abdomen oozing snakes, Pappy seized the chance to end this conversation.

"Well, I've got some fences to mend. I'll check back in later."

"Thanks, Pappy, I'd appreciate that."

I don't think we have enough fences to account for all Pappy's mending. What is he really spending so much time on? Rachel wondered, and then answered her own question; *probably his new young wife.*

The first time she had met Pappy, she remembered, he had really been repairing a fence. Shaman had called him over and introduced him as "my favorite cowboy and Indian."

Short, even by Hopi standards, and probably weighing less than her 120 pounds, Pappy had looked almost childlike, ambling across the graveled drive, his hair, as always, hanging loose under a bandanna. Like her own, it was as dark today as it had been nearly four decades ago.

Without warning, Rachel's mind wove the dark stands of hair into a disturbing vision. She imagined Pappy's head, mounted on a spear, his long hair reaching to the ground and beyond. The dark strands suddenly became a bottomless hole that was sucking Shaman and Zoe into its blackness. The phone rang. Rachel shook herself to dislodge the distressing vision and gratefully reached for the phone.

"Hello." Please let it be Shaman, she prayed.

"Rachel, this is Clyde."

"Oh Clyde, I'm so glad you called."

She really was glad to hear the familiar deep voice. Clyde was someone with whom she could share her fears. He wouldn't laugh at her vision. He would listen with his penetrating black eyes, not just his ears, while his ebony-crowned head nodded to show you that your words mattered.

"I've just had a frightening vision, Clyde. Shaman and Zoe are off searching for the sipapu hole, and I think they've found it. I know they're in danger."

"You've just saved me a lot of time angling for an invitation," Clyde said quickly. "I'll be there as soon as I can. I have a couple of Pillsbury dough boys in the waiting room—Clyde thought of most Caucasians as slug white and soft-headed—but it won't take me long to get rid of them. I'll call before I land at the old airstrip. We'll sort it out."

He hung up. After holding the receiver a minute longer, Rachel did the same. Somehow, she felt better just touching the receptacle that had carried his voice.

CHAPTER VI

Underworld

To Zoe it felt like a dream in which she'd jump from the top of the staircase and float rapidly toward the bottom. It was almost like flying, but they were flying down, not up, into a black hole where all light has been imploded.

Just as in her staircase dream, Zoe didn't remember landing, but she knew they had stopped falling. She moved her arms and legs, testing each limb. She couldn't feel any pain. Everything seemed to be working properly. Something scurried nearby. Zoe reached a trembling hand toward the blackness. A cold hand took hers, but no one spoke.

"Wher-where are we?" she stammered through her fright.

"You are at the beginning," a soft voice answered from the darkness.

"Are you the guide, Alo?" Zoe asked.

"Yes."

A faint aura of light now surrounded the strange Indian woman, and Zoe could see her grandfather. He was very close but he was not moving. She reached out her other hand, pulling it back quickly when she felt something crawl across it. She could hear what sounded like a great horde of writhing insects on both sides of the path where she sat.

Some of those closest to Alo she identified easily, for the polluted world in which she lived had been kinder to insects than animals. Zoe saw ladybugs and giant slugs. There were flies and ants, gnats and beetles, water bugs and roaches, and many she couldn't even name. It looked like every imaginable species, feeding upon one another in a cauldron of chaos. Thanks to a short academic course on insects, Zoe was not prone to panic at the sight of one, but she much preferred them in smaller numbers.

"I think I'm glad it's dark here," she murmured. "Are there many more of these things down here?"

"Listen," was all the guide replied.

Zoe did listen, and she could hear insect sounds coming from everywhere, even overhead. It was an insect cacophony. Only the path itself was untouched by some form of seething life.

"Did we really find the sipapu hole?" Zoe asked. "Is this the place where Sotuknang first planted his insects deep beneath the Earth?"

"What do you recall of your grandfather's story of creation, Zoe?" asked Alo.

"Well, according to one legend," Zoe began, "in the beginning there was only endless space, the mind of the Creator. Then the Creator made Sotuknang and commanded him to mold nine universes from this space," recited Zoe. "Sotuknang made water and air for the universes, and laid it all out according to a cosmic harmony."

"What happened next?" Alo prompted.

"Then, he created life from the center of the First World." Zoe digressed from her story, "I think that might be where we are." She looked again at those insects closest to them. "I don't really have anything against bugs, but I'd like to go home now."

"Please finish the story for me," Alo entreated.

Zoe couldn't take her eyes off the insects. Are they getting closer? "I'd really rather go home." No matter how hard Zoe strained her eyesight, she could see nothing beyond the small circle of Alo's glow and, right now, that was all right with her.

"Please, Zoe, continue." Alo's words were softly spoken but insistent.

Since talking left less room for fright, Zoe continued. "Animals came next. Then Spider Woman gathered earth and mixed it with saliva and shaped men and women. She covered the forms with her cape, and when she removed the cape, they came to life. But a spot on top of their heads stayed damp. That's how they could talk with their Creator."

"That's very good, Zoe," said Alo.

"How do you know my name?"

"I've been around a long time, my dear. I know a lot of things. Do you remember any more of the story?" Zoe was beginning to forget about the insects. She was glad no more had touched her.

"As people got smarter, they moved closer to the surface, until they finally climbed through the sipapu hole. When they reached the sunlight, it dried up the soft spot on their heads. Some of them forgot about the Creator and stopped performing the sacred rituals that kept the universe in harmony, so the Creator destroyed the whole world. He just saved those who had kept the 'doors on the top of their heads' open until he could make a Second World for them."

"Is that the end of the story?" asked Alo.

"Pretty much, this was repeated a couple more times, so we're on the Fourth World already," Zoe finished her story. At her back, Shaman began to stir.

"Are you all right, Zoe? Where we are?"

"I can't tell, Grandpa, but we have a guide. Her name is Alo. Don't move too fast. We're in some sort of insect nest."

I guess we're about to find out what the other night was all about, thought Shaman. He looked at the ground where they sat and noticed crystals reflecting the faint aura that encircled the guide. By their light, Shaman became aware of the multitude of insects surrounding them.

This is the beginning, and I'm actually seeing the first embryos of life. We're in the womb of Mother Earth.

As Alo began to move, Shaman's eyes picked out differing shades of darkness. Some took on solid contours further down the path. Zoe noticed them, too.

"Look, Grandpa. What are those things? They look like anthills."

Several shadowy creatures moved to and fro between the dark shapes that resembled huge anthills. These eerie figures moved with the precision of sightless bats through a complicated maze; shadows weaving among darker shadows.

"They're very scary," whispered Zoe.

Alo motioned for them to follow. Shaman straightened up slowly. He could hear the incessant humming of the insects very near his ears. Preferring not to proffer his hair as additional living space for whatever was buzzing above him, he remained stooped over. As they proceeded toward a tunnel opening, he noticed a platoon of ants drilling to some inner cadence known only to them and their instructors.

Shaman was anxious to leave this place. Before reaching the tunnel opening, Alo turned to him and asked cryptically,

"What lesson have you learned here that might light the path ahead?" Zoe looked at Shaman. He was at a loss.

"I have no idea what you're talking about, and standing here in a half-crouch does not improve my ability to think on my feet. Everyone is supposed to have an inner eye of knowledge that makes it possible to see in the dark, but if I have one, it must be blind," he admitted. He looked back toward the deafening nest of insects and squirming larvae. The only thing between there and here were the shadowy figures accompanying the marching ants. *What have I learned in this dark, chaotic place?* Suddenly, he knew the answer. He thought aloud. "Order must come from chaos before progress can be made."

"I can see that you were well chosen," said Alo.

Zoe wondered just what they had been chosen for. She recalled stories of ancient burial sites with mutilated human remains, a body cut in half and sewn back together, or bodies with no limbs and limbs with no bodies. Zoe was sure she did not want to be chosen for anything she did not volunteer for.

Once again, Alo was beckoning them to follow. The path was slightly better lit. Welcoming the added visibility, Shaman tried to get a better look at Alo, but her face remained elusive. She was hardly taller than Zoe. In the indigo hair knots over her ears, she wore hairdressings much like some he had found in old Anasazi burial sites.

Before he could speculate further on the identity of their guide, Alo indicated that they were to pass through the opening to the "Changing World."

"Stay to the path. Do not wander. If all goes well, I shall meet you some way down the trail. Then I will know if you are ready to continue." With those remarks, Alo was gone, and Zoe and Shaman were alone for the first time since their extraordinary entrance through the sipapu hole. When he looked back, Shaman could no longer see the tunnel through which they had just passed.

CHAPTER VII

The Journey Begins

———❦———

"Where did Alo go?" Zoe asked.

"I don't know." Shaman stared at the spot where Alo had been standing. He studied the surrounding area as far as he could see. "Stay close to me, Zoe. There are a lot of animal tracks on this trail."

Zoe slid her small hand inside of her grandfather's, and he gave it a reassuring squeeze. At least now he could stand up straight, and he could see a little more clearly. Since there was no other explanation for the sudden light source, Shaman assumed it must be radiating from that mysterious inner-eye. With the additional illumination, what he could make out was not very reassuring.

Murky shadows from rocky apertures gave him a feeling of being watched by hidden eyes. Numerous animal tracks suggested that any number of creatures might be lurking in those shadows.

"Can you read the tracks, Grandpa?"

"Some of them look like a big jackrabbit has been by recently, and just ahead are badger marks. I'll bet those that look like they were made by little pigs' feet are surely Havelina." He avoided mentioning the mountain lion, bear and sidewinder whose tracks were also unmistakable.

"These prints look like an animal was dragging its weight on malformed limbs." Shaman indicated some marks near their path. Then he pointed to more tracks just ahead. "I've never seen a stride as long as those." Whatever was out there, he intended to approach it with a great deal of caution. Alo's last words echoed in Shaman's mind. *Stay to the path.*

The uphill trail made Zoe's legs ache. She wished she were small enough to be carried. She remembered how her dad used to carry her on his shoulders when she was little. She could still feel her father's last hug before she left for a visit to her grandparents two years ago. A gentle and soft-spoken mountain of a man, he had enfolded her in his great arms, kissed her cheek, and whispered,

"I love you, have a wonderful adventure."

She never saw him again. Before Zoe returned, her parents, brother, and most of their neighbors had been claimed by a virulent strain of Nogales Flu. The Spanish influenza pandemic of 1918 paled by comparison before a treatment could be found. Only isolated areas had been spared near annihilation. It was but one of many puzzles confronting modern-day scientists in their never-ending battle with rampaging strains of bacteria and viruses.

At first Zoe had rejected the truth. She packed her bags and pretended that every day was the day before her departure, keeping out only the clothes she would need tomorrow, until, one day, the loneliness wasn't quite as intense. That morning Zoe put a few of her clothes back in her closet. Each day she took another item from her suitcases. Eventually the cases were empty, and the ranch had become her home.

Her grandparents had shared her grief. The death of their daughter and her family had left a void that could not be filled. They understood Zoe's need to delay the inevitable, that she would never see her family again.

As much as she loved Rachel and Shaman, Zoe still missed her mom and dad and brother. She closed her eyes to hold back the tears that threatened as the emerging young woman gave way to the lonely child inside. Shaman noticed that Zoe's steps had slowed.

"Why don't we sit here for a spell, Honey?" he suggested. "I'm getting a little tired."

"Me, too," she replied and plopped down in the middle of the path.

Shaman cradled his granddaughter in his arms and watched her eyelids dam the threatening flood. He felt a fiercely protective surge of love.

The voice said I am needed. It didn't say anything about Zoe. Where in God's name are we? Shaman held Zoe a little closer and stared intently at the surrounding shadows. *Just take things in order,* he calmed himself. *There must be a reason why we're here. Just keep your composure.*

We were looking for the sipapu hole. I think we may have found it. Just before reality was replaced by something like "Alice-in-Wonderland's" rabbit hole, I was telling Zoe a Hopi story of creation. If we are, indeed, in the legendary Underworld, I might find a clue to our escape in the Hopi tales of the emergence of their ancestors.

Shaman scanned the path for any further signs of life and tried to remember all he could about the scant artifacts left by the Hisatsinom. They told a story of accomplished architects and farmers who often congregated in pueblo villages. He ran through his mental catalog of medicine bags, ceremonial objects, pottery, tools and idols which those villages had relinquished for his research.

He remembered some more gruesome finds, as well. One particularly grisly find was a body with the face of some other poor soul hung from the neck. Were these the barbaric relics of an ancient law that demanded severe penalties for breaking the rules of its society? With the question, came fear, like a maggot nibbling at his consciousness. Shaman was reminded that Hopi retribution can be swift and deadly.

He kept an eye out for anything that might be loping, crawling, or slithering through the dark shadows surrounding their little oasis of light as he recalled the Hopi ritual of the "Night of the Washing of the Hair." This night the initiates to the religious societies are secluded in the kivas to protect them from the contamination of evil powers. All roads to the village are closed by drawing a line across them with sacred cornmeal. Only the road to the burial grounds remains open to allow the ancestral spirits to roam the streets. Any human intruder caught in the village could be killed and dismembered by the sentries. Recalling this made Shaman resolve to avoid unintentional transgression.

"What the hell is that?" Sham muttered. The subject of his expletive, skittering away on the right of their path, appeared to be a very large beetle with furry ears and a cottontail. Another strange creature revealed itself on the other side of the path. This one was dashing about in frantic circles, like a large puppy chasing its own tail, but it most certainly was not a puppy. It looked like a jackrabbit. However, there was a striking difference. Its head was that of a coyote.

Zoe started at Shaman's short outburst.

"Oh, Grandpa, what are they?" Entranced, she stared at first one and then the other.

"Poor thing," said Zoe. "If that coyote rabbit ever catches itself, it'll be a painful lesson." As though hearing the reference to its self, the newly named coyote rabbit hopped to the edge of the trail. It snarled viciously at the interlopers, adding impetus to their immediate wish to be further down the path. At that moment, a familiar looking white dog came loping up beside them. The dog was more than a match for the coyote rabbit. Raised hackles and a low, meaningful growl were enough to send the strange creature into the shadows. Before Sham could speak, Zoe gave the dog an affectionate pat on the head. To Sham's relief, it was once more the placid guard who had attached itself to Zoe at the hotel.

"Good boy, Charlie." Shaman rewarded the animal with a pat of his own. Zoe was very pleased to see her friend again. Shaman allowed her to romp with the pet while he worked at retrieving more Anasazi information from his mental file. After a few moments, Shaman asked,

"Zoe, do you remember the part of the creation story when Spider Grandmother was sent to lead the insects nearer to the Earth's surface?"

"Sure, that's where animals first appeared."

"So, this Changing World could be the next level of creation, and the coyote rabbit has not yet completed its metamorphosis," Shaman speculated aloud.

"Well," Zoe volunteered, "no wonder it acts vicious. It's probably really confused, having to chase itself all the time. When it becomes either a rabbit or a coyote, it will know what to do. I hope it happens soon, before it ends up eating itself."

"You make a good point, Zoe. The dog knows it is a dog and is content to be a companion. An animal with no direction can be a dangerous thing. I believe an animal, or a person, must understand itself before it knows how to relate to others." Shaman had no sooner said this than he found Alo standing at their side where only moments before the dog had been nuzzling Zoe's hand.

"Your wisdom shortens your journey, but there is still far to go, and the lessons will get harder. Let's be on our way," Alo instructed and moved ahead.

Shaman noticed that the brightness of Alo's aura was diminishing as his ability to see improved. As she led them once again toward an entrance to whatever lay beyond, Shaman's previous attention turned to irritation. He felt patronized. Given the circumstances presented, the so-called lessons were no more than logical assumptions. *For heaven's sake, I'm an anthropologist, not a child.* As these thoughts bubbled to the surface of Sham's consciousness, Alo came to an abrupt halt.

"We'll rest here for a few moments," she informed them.

Still smarting from his imagined mistreatment, Sham sat next to Zoe and nursed his resentment. Soon he was overcome by lethargy. He only vaguely heard Alo addressing him.

"Now you must begin a separate journey. You and the child have much to learn. What you have lost, she must discover. When you wake, you will find a new path. Follow it ever upward. If you prove worthy of being chosen, you will again find your Zoe before you reach the summit. Rest now, for your way will be most difficult."

Sham dreamt that he was maneuvering a four-wheel drive up a precipitous trail, and he was bone-tired. Tires spinning, he fought for control. Ahead was a narrow, rocky, hairpin curve. The view was of limitless sky, broken only by the shadow of a wayward cloud stealing the light from a harvest moon. The excuse for a road evidenced no guard rails. There was nothing to impede a vehicle from driving straight out into beckoning space.

He had just begun to negotiate the sharp turn when the siren cloud seduced his concentration, and he dozed off behind the wheel.

In a fraction of a second, he was awakened by a gentle hand shaking his shoulder. He turned to the passenger seat, where his mother sat, smiling. In her usual school-morning voice she said, "Wake up, sleepy head."

Sham braked the car to a screeching halt, within inches of driving over the edge of a two-thousand-foot drop into oblivion. When he turned again to the seat beside him, his mother was gone.

As his eyes snapped to attention, Sham heard her voice. "Get up, Shaman. You must get on with the task before you. You are needed."

CHAPTER VIII

Anxiety furrowed Clyde's brow. Rachel had sounded terrified on the phone. What kind of danger were Shaman and Zoe in? The universe is full of danger—some real, some surreal; either could be deadly. He must get to the ranch as quickly as possible. He pressed the intercom.

"Yes sir."

"You can send them in now."

Clyde appraised his new clients as they entered the office. Mutt and Jeff, he thought. In spite of the burn bandages, the tall one grabbed Clyde's hand and pumped it like a jack-handle.

"Thanks for taking our case, man. We know you're the best. Nobody shoulda been in that boarded-up building. We just couldn't save them four roaches."

Four derelicts dead by arson, just roaches to this animal, a small price to pay to open a city block to redevelopment. If we still used the electric chair, I might just let these Pillsbury bastards fry. Nice little euphemism we use today, put to sleep. It sounds like a compassionate vet putting a favorite pet out of its misery. These two guilty slugs aren't domesticated enough to be pets. They're more like rabid wolves.

"Before I'm through, the jury will be convinced that you two were good Samaritans trying to save the homeless from becoming toast. We're talking seven figures for my fee. Can you handle that?" The little one pulled a bank draft from his inside coat pocket.

"I think this will cover any costs that might arise." Clyde recognized the coded account number. These two had some heavy-weight backers.

"Thank you, gentlemen, I'm on a very tight schedule today, but my assistant will set up your next appointment." He held the door until Mutt and Jeff made their way to his assistant's desk just beyond, then let his thoughts return to Shaman. Sham was the only white man he'd ever had much use for. Of course, Sham wasn't one hundred percent White, and with that overstated humbleness, he could have been a full-blooded Hopi.

He tried to remember one controversial thing Sham had ever done. It was a long empty minute. Shaman could always blend in wherever he happened to be. Clyde, on the other hand, knew that he would never be completely accepted by either of his parents' tribes or the predominately Caucasian inhabitants of the world of jurisprudence.

At all of the Hopi gatherings, he knew that they were not as comfortable with his presence as they would have been if his father were not Navaho. The same was true of his father's tribe. They were painfully conscious of his Hopi lineage. Under the circumstances, Clyde was most at home in the company of his blood-brother.

Clyde relived the excitement of that solemn occasion when he and Sham had mixed their blood. He felt the warm fluid streaming as the knife made its way across his palm. He thrilled to the surge of power that quickened his pulse as his pony sliced a path through the wind, his own blood painting the side of the galloping horse.

Thank the Creator that Sham has outlived the new mortality rate. Clyde tallied all the friends he had lost over the decades. *There were damn few left. A man needs someone to toast the good old days with. Memories need to be shared once in a while with someone who's been there. Shaman is that someone for me.* Clyde pressed the intercom.

"I'm leaving now. Clear my calendar for the next few days. If you have to, you can reach me at the Thomas Ranch." He dashed out the back entrance and raced to the automobile waiting in his private space.

Clyde all but ejected from the car when it skidded to a stop. He climbed the stairs by threes, threw clothes at an open suitcase—whatever hit the case traveled—and within minutes, he was on his way to his own airstrip. A few minutes more and he was streaking across the sky, headed due west.

The thrill of flying was much like racing across an open plain on a high-strung stallion. The plane was trustworthy and powerful and in his control. This was one of those times—and there were many—when he really enjoyed being rich. He must get to Shaman.

CHAPTER IX

Separated

When Shaman awoke, Zoe had vanished. He was alone on a stony path made up of the residue from the solid rock at his back. Ahead, he saw two trails. One reached out straight and level with a promise of easy traveling. The other inclined steeply, foreboding aching calves and back.

Frantic to find Zoe, he chose the path that promised the most speed. Less than a dozen strides down the trail, he remembered the words Alo had whispered just before he had dozed off. "Follow it upward."

Had he chosen the wrong avenue? He turned to retrace his steps. To his surprise, there was again only solid rock at his back. He had no choice but to proceed along the level path.

How was he to find Zoe? He thought of his granddaughter, exceptionally bright, on the verge of becoming a young lady but still wrapped in a tender cocoon of childishness. When he looked into Zoe's eyes his mother's eyes stared back at him, reminding him that the universe is a continuum whose parts cannot be separated. A low droning voice broke into his thoughts. Ahead, Shaman could just make out the form of someone squatting on the edge of the path.

"Hello, friend," Shaman addressed the form. "Were you speaking to me?"

The squatting figure slowly turned its wrinkled face toward him. Sham couldn't tell if it was male or female. The head, shoulders, and torso were totally covered by a shawl. The wrinkled features gave away nothing but age. A mere one hundred years could not have produced the deep, fleshy crevices of forehead, cheek, and jowl which bespoke antiquity.

"I was remembering. Were you listening?" Sound escaped the ancient lips like dusty drafts from a long closed tomb.

"I'm sorry, I didn't catch the words, just your voice," Sham apologized.

"If you want to hear, you must listen. It has been a long while since I told a story." Sham almost felt guilty for having thoughts of his own that interfered with the old relic's words.

"Are you a storyteller, then?"

"Are you a listener?" asked the relic.

"At the moment, I'm just a wanderer. I'm looking for my granddaughter. Did a young girl recently come this way?

"I haven't seen the girl, but I can tell you a story."

Sham squatted next to the old narrator and gave his undivided attention, for he was sure that nothing that happened here was a coincidence. The story could be the clue to finding Zoe. The storyteller began.

Her name was Laughing Flower, and she was the daughter of their leader, Clawing Bear. She was everything her name implied: beautiful as a saguaro flower, with a happy spirit that brought joy to all her clan.

Laughing Flower had reached the age of adding to the clan's numbers. Each month her moon cycle brought a new fullness to her body, readying her to participate in the cycle of life. All the young men now paid her a different kind of attention. She was no longer just a laughing child. She had lost her desire to enter the children's circle with the others to leap and run and imitate their animal family.

Lately, a more enjoyable pastime for Laughing Flower was stealing glances at the young men who were honing their skills with spears and clubs. These glances fell most often upon Running Creek, the father of her sister's children. She loved to watch the muscles strain in his arms and chest and thighs when he ran faster and threw his spear farther than anyone else. But most of all, she loved to look upon his face. To Laughing Flower, it was the face of a god.

Some nights she would hear her sister and Running Creek making noises of enjoyment as their covering hides rose and fell in syncopation. She wondered what it would be like to share those hides with Running Creek. She knew that this was not allowed, for no male had been permitted to father children of more than one woman since the People had survived the great shaking of the Earth.

Laughing Flower could still hear the screams of the children who had been flung into steaming crevices. Frantic mothers had grasped their youngest babies to their breasts, tied themselves to giant trees, and stared helplessly into the eyes of those youngsters they could not reach. Young men dashed to the children's circle, grabbed any they could reach and sought solid footing. Many young braves, along with the terrified youngsters in their arms, were thrown into the steaming rivers beneath the Earth. When those who had been hunting returned, they found the children and young males much fewer in number. Most of the survivors were the mothers and their youngest offspring.

After that calamity, by rule of the clan's elders, each male could father the children of only one woman. The children, as soon as they were old enough, were taught to harness themselves to long strips of rawhide that were attached to giant trees if the earth began to shake. The Earth had not quaked since that time, so the people were sure that the elders' rule was good.

Running Creek had also noticed the growing beauty of Laughing Flower. When he caught her glancing his way, he would inhale deeper, bunching his already impressive muscles, enjoying the admiration on her face. His spear flew farther and he ran faster when she was around, but he knew the terrible punishment for breaking an elders' rule.

Laws were not made lightly and were usually prompted by a great calamity when man upset the harmony of nature. Even so, he could not prevent himself from fathering a child of this lovely maiden. They stole many hours to be alone in the great forest before it was obvious to them both that Laughing Flower would soon be bearing his child. This impending event did not go unnoticed by the elders.

Since no male had yet approached the council and offered to hunt for Laughing Flower, thus earning the right to father children by her, it was apparent that the elders' rule had been broken. The guilty party must be punished, or the Earth in its anger might destroy them all.

When questioned concerning the identity of the father of her unborn child, Laughing Flower did not lie. The same was true of Running Creek. He had broken an elders' rule, and must accept responsibility for his actions and bear the punishment for his offense.

People were expected to conduct themselves in a manner which contributed to the well-being of the cosmic whole. Nature could be a hard taskmaster, obliterating whole villages by fire, famine, or pestilence. With so much at stake, punishment for transgression was harsh and swift.

After the setting of four suns, Clawing Bear called a council of the elders. All the young males who had not yet approached the council to select a mother for their future children were gathered in the village circle. From those who stepped forth, the elders proceeded to choose two strong young males to be honored with the duty of fathering the two sisters' offspring.

Next, Running Creek was commanded to come forward. His sentence was quick and terrifying. He must throw himself into the boiling geyser that spewed hot mud on the surrounding earth. His clan would escort him on this journey, but Running Creek knew that he was expected to carry out his own punishment. If he forced the People to throw him into the pit, it would dishonor his name forever.

That night, a feast was prepared so all the villagers could say good-bye to Running Creek. As the sun rose on the horizon, they accompanied him to the place of retribution. There, without a word, Running Creek climbed onto a nearby outcropping. After turning once to lock his eyes with those of Laughing Flower, he dove headfirst into the boiling pit. The people had done their duty and sadly returned to the village.

Laughing Flower pined for the sight of Running Creek's beautiful face and fell into a deep depression. When she went into labor, it lasted for three days before the child was stillborn. The shaman was unable to save Laughing Flower, who wished only to join her infant son. The villagers bid farewell to the one who gave them joy, and laying her stillborn infant in her arms, they carried them tenderly to their final resting place.

The burial grounds were beyond the bubbling cauldron, and as the people paraded past, carrying their burdens, a cry from the last in the procession held them in their tracks. Clawing Bear had discovered, lying on the Earth and looking like nothing so much as a newly cured hide, the face of Running Creek. It had been boiled from the bone and spewed forth from the bubbling cauldron. Running Creek had retained his honor and had been returned to his people. Clawing Bear picked up the piece of boiled skin and attached it like a necklace to his beloved Laughing Flower so the three of them could be laid to rest together.

The tale finished, the old narrator stood and moved slowly into the shadows and disappeared in an instant.

Shaman thought about the story.

It clears up the mystery of the skeleton with the mummified face around its neck. Many historians had tried to explain that Anasazi grave, but no one had ever come up with an acceptable theory.

It was certainly a warning that transgression against nature's laws demands a sacrifice. *Surely Zoe hasn't violated any laws. Sins of the fathers? The children on Earth are already paying a heavy price for those. Could Zoe be the ultimate sacrifice?*

CHAPTER X

Introspection

Suddenly Sham felt an icy wind, and all his childhood fears were snapping at his heels. His mind was transported to those cowboy and Indian matinees that sometimes left him feeling anxious for days. He could hear the sounds of drums and wild howling that usually preceded some torture; a trespasser being flayed alive or tied between bent saplings, to be torn in two when the saplings were released or, perhaps, an offender whose eyelids had been sewn open before being staked in the desert sun over a red ant hill.

These were only the first Hollywood scripts which readily came to mind; scenes he had spent his Saturday afternoons as a child watching on a wide movie screen, followed by Saturday nights huddled in bed, fearing every shadow thrown across his room by the headlights of passing automobiles.

The chill grew in intensity. A great chasm opened before him. He peered into its depths and felt the accumulated terror of all those Saturday nights. The remorseful cries of hundreds of ghosts who had violated ancient creeds assaulted his ears. He saw the mutilated remains of all those who had paid the price for those transgressions. The scope of devastation grew to proportions beyond comprehension.

Shaman stood transfixed, engulfed by unrelenting sorrow for man's capacity for desecration. He became one with the Earth, bruised and scarred from the torturous treatment at the hands of those she sought to succor. Her life-giving waters flowed as sluggishly as congealing blood. The winds screamed her pain for all to hear, but no one listened.

Shaman began to weep. What had he done to try to save the Earth? Worn a few paltry "Save the Whales" shirts? Or testified, calmly and reasonably, at a Senate hearing or two to preserve a few acres of sacred land, recycled?

"It wasn't enough," he berated himself for his own passivity.

As the hot tears cleared his vision, the chasm of mayhem faded away. In its place stood a wizened old Indian, holding a hardwood spear with a stone tip. The tiny man was at least a foot shorter than the six-foot-long weapon. His hair was short on top but fell down his back in a long queue, which was wound about with an elaborate hairdressing. His only clothing was a blanket of animal hide and a pair of fiber sandals. Riveting Shaman with a piercing gaze, the startling apparition proclaimed.

"You are the namesake of the Great Shaman. You have chosen this path, and you have seen the pit of evil. What is the truth?"

"The truth is, I expected the world to take care of itself while I picked at its skin and puttered in its scars. For the most part, I avoided the battles, leaving it to others to fight for the Earth that sustained me. I never aggressively walked a picket line, challenged a whaling boat, or pounded on the door of the Senate.

"I even accepted the death of my parents passively, leaving it to others to find the answers and accepting their failure without question. Somehow passive felt like righteous."

"It is not easy to change one's nature," said Sham's inquisitor, "but this is your hour of redemption. If you have forgotten the old ways, you will join those who wait for a worthy one to rid the world of tyrants. If you are wise, you will use the past to save yourself and continue on the upward path of knowledge." The old seer brandished his spear, and Shaman was once again alone, surrounded by hundreds of snakes. *My God, every snake indigenous to Arizona must be represented in this tangled collection!*

In all directions, they slithered, slept, or rolled on the now sandy terrain. He identified gopher snakes and sidewinders, harmless racers and bull snakes, as well as poisonous rattlers. There were deadly coral snakes and the venom-less great king snake, nearly identical in coloring.

About four feet away, a large diamondback began to coil and speared him with its slitted eye. Even knowing that a coiled snake cannot spring farther than the distance of its own length, he was sure the space between them would not save him if the rattler chose to strike.

Ahead, the level path began a steep climb toward his only hope for escape. A few yards beyond, below a rocky shelf, he could just make out a long, narrow opening where the shelf's column met the tunnel wall. Another quick look dashed his hopes of finding anything he could use to vault beyond the reptiles. There was no weapon at hand—not even a forked stick. The only object he could see was an ancient water jar protruding from the middle of the path. An exceptionally large viper with a peculiar red underbelly twined around the base of this jar.

The snakes slithered nearer. The diamondback continued to coil. Shaman fought the numbing terror that tried to paralyze his brain. Concentrate, he admonished himself.

"We aren't going to hurt each other, are we, big fellow," he said in a conciliatory tone. *What did that old wizard say? Use the past to save myself.*

He dredged from his memory the legend of Tiyo, son of the village chief of Tokoonavi. Tiyo married Tcuamana from the Underworld, who had the knowledge to prevent death from rattlesnake bite. At the wedding ceremonies, when the Snake people from the Underworld had been transformed into venomous reptiles, Tcuamana instructed Tiyo's people to wash the heads of the reptiles and dance with them to render the vipers harmless. The water jar must be the key to survival!

Before fear could overpower this recollection, Shaman lunged toward the large snake. Just as the red-bellied viper reached eye level with the opening of the jar, Sham grasped it behind its menacing head and forced the head into the cleansing water. Before the undulating, massive reptile could twine about his body, Sham emptied the jar of water upon the snakes barring his path, and danced quickly toward the welcoming crevice. Here he saw a single fluffy eagle's feather lying in the middle of his path.

Shaman laid the now harmless snake aside and picked up the feather before entering the dark opening to whatever lay beyond. He knew that a paho, a prayer-feather, could fly messages to the heavens and might be of great benefit to him on this strange journey. He placed the feather into the emptied jar and knelt to catch his breath.

The level path had certainly turned out to be a most difficult one. Taking the easy way had sent him rushing headlong down the wrong trail and had nearly cost his life.

If I die now, what hope will there be for Zoe?

CHAPTER XI

Enlightenment

Zoe and Alo were standing in a beautiful clearing surrounded by large trees. Zoe couldn't remember leaving her grandfather, but she was not frightened. She ran through the flowery meadow. Downy petals floated everywhere as she fell in a bed of clover and gazed up through the branches of an enormous evergreen into a brilliant blue sky. Such color! She inhaled the crystal air and felt the warmth of a sunlit day. She was so captivated by the marvelous sky that she barely noticed the leather thongs attached to the trunks of the tree.

There were animals everywhere. Squirrels played hide-and-seek between the tree branches. Soft, furry rabbits capered in the meadow. Butterflies of every description splashed like raindrops on the petals.

"Where are we? This place is so beautiful!"

"We are where the world remains as it should be," replied Alo.

In her thirteen years, Zoe had seen a few days when the sun's rays briefly pierced the gray barrier of pollution, but this was like stepping into a golden page of one of her precious books.

"How could people let a world like this turn into the one we live in today?" she asked.

"That is a good question, Zoe."

The trickle of running water caught Zoe's attention. In search of the stream that sounded like bubbling laughter, she wandered deeper into the magnificent forest. Soon she came upon a small pool shimmering in the sun's reflection.

"Look over there, Zoe," Alo whispered, pointing to a small fawn drinking from the pool. "See its mother standing guard?" Zoe spied a soft-eyed doe, nearly hidden by the surrounding foliage, its ears sharply alert to any possible danger.

"Oh, she's wonderful!" Zoe exclaimed, causing the deer to bolt and call her fawn back to the protection of the deeper woods. As the doe and its fawn disappeared into the trees, Zoe heard an unfamiliar sound.

"What's all that noise?"

"It's your welcoming committee," Alo answered.

Zoe looked up at the tall pine branches and saw brilliantly colored birds chirping in chorus. The trilling sound of their serenade accompanied her as she turned back to the little lake where white butterflies decorated the mosses growing on the rocks above the pool. Clear water, like ballerinas dancing center stage, rushed between the rocks; pirouette, then bow in unison into a sea of silver ruffles.

The sound of voices pierced Zoe's consciousness. She looked up to see a small group of children coming toward her. They were dressed in softened hides and carried empty baskets woven into intricate designs. When the children saw Zoe, they stopped their chatter and waited some distance away. Alo motioned for them to approach. The children's chatter was replaced by squeals of delight as they rushed to her side.

"I see you are off to pick berries," Alo said, patting and hugging first this one, then another. "Take Zoe along with you. Teach her how to tell which ones are edible and which will make her tummy ache. Just make sure you save a few for dinner."

Zoe was soon picking berries with this group of youngsters and feeling quite at home. She had eaten so many berries that her basket was less than half full. She had never tasted anything so sweet. This fruit needed no flavor enhancing to make it palatable. She wondered if all food had tasted this good when it could be grown in sunshine, with unpurified rain water.

As she hurried to fill her basket, Zoe looked at the trees and thought of the towering incinerators that dotted the landscape in the world she was familiar with; a world where lush acreage like this had once provided lavish gardens and parks. But that was before landfills contaminated water tables with toxic wastes. The incinerators that replaced the landfills only added to the problem of air pollution.

For more than Zoe's short lifetime, the world's food supply had been dependent on artificial production. Berries grown in chemicals, under artificial sunlight, could never compare to these. She couldn't wait to try some other foods, though it might be a few hours before her full stomach would agree.

As the children prepared to return home with their baskets, a young brave approached, carrying a bow and a quiver of arrows. As he disappeared into the forest to hunt for the evening meal, Zoe gave her half-full basket to one of the children and set out after the hunter. They had not gone very deeply into the forest before a lone deer stepped from behind a large tree trunk. It stood very still, and much to Zoe's surprise, the animal spoke.

"I have come to grace your fire tonight. Shoot swiftly and true," Zoe heard the deer implore. The young man drew an arrow and placed it across his bow. His arrow was indeed true to its mark, dropping the animal where it stood. As he recovered the deer, the hunter thanked its spirit for its sacrifice. He quickly found a long stick, tied the carcass to it, and began dragging it back toward the berry patch.

Zoe stepped from behind the tree where she had been observing the hunter, and squeamishly picked up one end of the pole. The hind, though small, was heavier than she had imagined. She stooped beneath the pole and raised it across her shoulder and managed to heft its weight. The young brave smiled his thanks and led her to a gathering of people awaiting their return.

When others had taken the meat to prepare for the meal, Zoe turned to the young hunter and asked,

"Why would an animal allow itself to be slaughtered? And do all animals speak here?"

"Of course they do not speak as humans, but we understand them, nonetheless," said the hunter. "They know their place in the world. One of their duties is to feed the hungry."

"So they just let you shoot them?"

"They ask only that we take no more than we need, and they are appreciative of a swift death. We kill only what we need for food, and we thank them for their gifts because without them we could not survive. If we do not respect the animals, they will leave, and we shall have to abandon our beautiful village."

This seemed logical to Zoe. After all, it was more humane than that horrible vocational video she'd seen in which geese were being raised to make fois gras.

"I once saw geese whose feet had been nailed to the floor so their bodies would use up fewer calories. Through a funnel, they were force-fed huge amounts of corn. When sufficiently fattened, they were killed for their grossly enlarged livers. I have no interest in ever tasting fois gras," she told the astounded hunter.

Tonight Zoe ate corn that tasted of sunshine, venison so tender it melted on her tongue, and sweet golden cornmeal wrapped and cooked in flattened cornhusks. She also managed to eat just a few more of the juicy berries. As she experienced the sights and sounds of this unpolluted world, she wondered if her grandfather was having as wonderful an experience as she was enjoying. After dinner, Alo took Zoe to a bed of soft branches and even softer hides. Zoe was asleep before she could give any more thought to where her grandfather might be.

CHAPTER XII

Seedlings

The grey skies finally opened, and an ocean of rain strafed the roof in waves. Rachel felt, more than heard, the lightning strike. *Please, not the sun-panels.* She called to Pappy, but her voice was drowned by the booming thunder. She grabbed her rain-slicker and a flare before braving the torrent of liquid needles that pricked her exposed face and hands.

She made a quick assessment of the damages. The main sun-panels were still lit, but the small panels above the second tier were out. Those plants on the lower tier would have to be exposed to the remaining lights. Pappy saw the flare and raced to the seedling nursery. Rachel watched him approach. Was he loping or limping? Maybe he really wasn't well. Pappy lunged into the greenhouse and shook himself like a big dog.

"Did it get the panels?"

"No, but it took out the generator for the second tier. Until it's replaced, we'll have to move the lower shelves into the aisles. It's going to make for tight maneuvering. Are you OK, Pappy?" She watched him take a few steps. No limp now.

"I'm fine. My joints just get a little stiff."

"I can certainly sympathize with that. Some days my shadow even aches," Rachel empathized. Pappy cranked a pulley at one end of the greenhouse while Rachel did the same at the other end, and a hidden shelf of seedling pots slid from beneath another that was waist high.

"These plants are already stunted, waiting for the parts to fix the panels. They should have a foot more growth by now. They'd be this big if we started them in the field with whatever sunlight filtered through," pappy remarked disgustedly.

"Probably, but this cloudburst would have washed them away. They need a better root system to make it in the fields," Rachel pointed out. "With a few extra hours of artificial sunlight, they'll perk up quick enough. Thank goodness the lightning struck the small generator and not the panels."

Rachel edged her way past Pappy and the plants that now took up two-thirds of the aisle. She wrinkled her nose and tried unsuccessfully to control a sneeze.

"Bet you got soaked coming out here," Pappy said. "You better get back to the house. I can finish up here. Don't want you catching your death."

"For a minute there, I thought I smelled Mongrel. You know, I haven't sneezed since that old hound passed away," Rachel remarked.

"He sure did love to rut around in the greenhouses. And he hated rain. Maybe his old spirit came in to get dry." Pappy ushered Rachel out the door. She sloshed back to the house and settled herself with a cup of hot tea. She sipped the soothing brew, thankful that the seedlings were all right, and exhibited no more cold symptoms.

Now she had time to worry about Shaman and Zoe again. Was it raining where they were? In her vision, they had been in a deep hole of some kind. Had they fallen into a mine shaft? Were they in a cave? Had they really found the sipapu hole?

Rachel knew that her vision somehow related to Shaman's episode in the library. Well, Clyde would be here soon. Together they would have a better chance of locating Shaman and Zoe.

CHAPTER XIII

Inspiration

After his close call with the reptiles, Shaman took a deep breath. He looked at the shaking hand that had held the ugly snake's head. He sat down and folded his arms across his knees and rested his forehead on them.

Thank God Rachel didn't come. He couldn't bear to think of her in that snake pit he had just escaped. His wonderful Rachel, that inquiring mind and poet's soul dressed in satin skin and crowned with the blue-black hair that marked her ancestry. He pictured her marvelous figure that had only grown more womanly as their children and time added new dimensions to her body.

Desire overtook him as his physical body responded to his thoughts of Rachel. Eluding death by snakebite had left him feeling very much alive. He wanted to hold her and share this new passion for life. He wanted to feel once more the thrill of their wedding night, when they had cavorted like Adam and Eve in a world created for their pleasure, gathering branches, each aware of the other's touch as they prepared their nuptial bed in an ancient ruin.

Rachel's body had shone like alabaster in the starlight, almost too beautiful to touch. Finally, he pulled her to him, and the stars turned to fireworks as they experienced a unity of body and soul that they had never felt before. No aborigine was ever more closely attuned to another than were Rachel and he that night. On a windswept mesa, bodies and hearts bared to one another, their souls had soared as one to the celestial lights shining over their heads.

As if his need had called forth her essence, Shaman could feel Rachel's presence. He closed his eyes and touched the smooth skin of her face and smelled the fragrance of her favorite scent. His hands caressed the curves of her hips and her surprisingly firm breasts and those long legs that could hold him so tightly that he never wanted to be anywhere but there.

"You're a dirty old man, Shaman," said the laughing Rachel of his wishful dream, mimicking her bantering foreplay of their real world, teasing him about the few years of difference in their ages.

Was it only yesterday that he had held her and made love until they reached that simultaneous eruption of passion that always left them wrapped in contentment?

His dream-Rachel took his head in her lap and caressed his brow. Sham found solace in her imagined touch as the adrenalin rush subsided, and his mind drifted to a pleasant memory from his childhood.

❈　❈　❈

He had just turned thirteen and his folks had taken him on one of their many excursions to discover Arizona. They crossed a bridge spanning a dry wash near a small town called Wickenburg.

"Wow, look at all those flowers," exclaimed young Shaman. His dad pulled the car to the side of the road and parked next to a large meadow of desert blossoms.

Sham's mother picked a handful of wild purple lupine and gold mariposa lily, which she called butterfly, and put them in a jar to grace their picnic blanket. Sham's dad pointed to a nearby thicket. In its shadow, a small doe was leading her baby toward the sound of running water.

"Dad, why do they have a 'no fishing' sign on that bridge we passed?" Sham asked. He certainly didn't think anyone would need to be told not to waste their time fishing in a dry gulch.

"Well, Sham, that's the Hassayampa River. It's there, alright. You just can't see it."

"I don't see any river. You're kidding, aren't you, Dad?"

"No son, it's actually there. Where we crossed the bridge, the Hassayampa flows underground, but we'll be able to see it running on the surface just over here."

"We'll picnic by the river," suggested Sham's mother. "But we have to be careful. The story goes that if you drink from the Hassayampa, you'll never tell the truth again. It's a good thing we brought plenty of lemonade."

In a small oasis on the high desert, they moved cautiously past a large area of quicksand to a small green meadow. Here the Hassayampa emerged, running gleefully over the sandy river bottom, drinking in the sunshine for a few brief miles before carrying its hostage rays beneath the Earth.

Sham's dad was right, at least about where they would find the river. He didn't know about the rest of the story because he was very careful not to drink from the enchanted, disappearing stream. He lay in the shade of a large smoke tree and peered at the azure sky. There wasn't a cloud to be seen.

When his thoughts returned to the present, an aging Shaman realized how much he missed the Arizona of his youth. Even before the nuclear disaster, the usually cloudless skies had begun to darken. A few years after the turn of the century, those skies still lured sun-worshipers, the aged and ailing, and finally everyone who still remembered clean air and sunshine.

In the last half of the twentieth century, they had come with dreams and all the ills they thought they were leaving behind. The people arrived with gas-guzzling recreational vehicles, faster and more dangerous water craft, and the devastating all-terrain vehicle. They proceeded to destroy the land, water, and air at an unprecedented pace.

"These people are committing suicide by RV," Sham remembered his father saying, and the Thomas family increasingly avoided the more populated areas of Arizona. Sham was grateful that his parents had chosen a name that steered his own interests to earlier cultures with their simpler understanding of humanity's relationship to the environment.

"A name should be something one can wear with pride, like a favorite overcoat," he always stressed to his own family. He wondered now if Zoe would be guided in some way by her given name. Life, what a wonderful thing she is named for.

His own voice stirred Shaman from his reverie. He must get on with his journey. He put his thoughts of family aside. Though loathe to relinquish the comfort those thoughts had provided, he knew his ordeal was far from finished. He rose stiffly to his feet and forced himself to continue his quest.

CHAPTER XIV

Shaman's path again branched in two directions. To the left, the trail was enclosed within the walls of a narrow tunnel. To the right, blue-grey sagebrush and creosote bushes speckled desert grassland. Shaman resisted the claustrophobic walls to the left and quickly followed the open trail to his right.

Not far down the chosen fork, the grasslands disappeared. They had been replaced by some of the most inhospitable land Shaman had ever seen. Not even a cactus could be found struggling for survival in the rocky outcrops. Death Valley was no more desolate than what stretched before him.

The air grew hotter with each breath he took and sucked the fluids from his body. Sham decided that the narrow, walled path would be preferable to what lay ahead and turned to retrace his steps, only to find that the path behind had become no less desolate than the one ahead. He had made his choice and was compelled to plod forward into the arid wasteland.

Shaman's throat was parched, his tongue felt many times its normal size, and his skin itched from dryness. His eyes began to burn. His scalp prickled as though inhabited by pincer-wielding insects. He struggled on, looking for any sign of water on the harsh terrain. Shaman thought of a phrase his grandfather had often used. He could hear the old man's voice expounding.

"If you burned hell and sifted the ashes, you couldn't find worse than this." As Sham stared at the arid wasteland, the old phrase seemed most appropriate. A few more steps and he could travel no farther. He collapsed in a withered heap. His only thoughts were of Zoe. *I've failed her. What will become of her now?*

As he dropped to the burning sand, the jar fell by his side into a small depression in the ground. Until this moment, he had forgotten that he still carried it. The jar no sooner touched bottom than a few drops of crystal water began to form inside.

Shaman could hardly believe his eyes. In only seconds, there was a sufficient amount of liquid to slake his thirst and renew his ability to think. As the moisture revived his brain and reduced the size of his tongue, Shaman thanked the Creator that the Hopi story of the magic water jar was more than a myth.

He took one more drink of the purest water he had ever tasted, and saw the eagle's feather floating on the liquid contained within. He reached for the feather. His fingers cramped, and the sound of the miraculous jar shattering at his feet rang like a funeral dirge. Shaman wanted to cry, but he dared not waste the moisture if he was to survive any length of time along this parched trail.

When he turned to forge ahead the arid wasteland had been transformed. It rose more steeply now, but compared to the ordeal which he had just endured, Shaman was not worried about a few aching muscles. The air surrounding him was no longer intolerably hot, and the steeper path offered occasional roots to help pull him along. He climbed for some time before reaching the entrance to yet another tunnel.

Before entering the next stage of this bizarre journey Shaman decided to rest and reflect again upon his knowledge of ancient Indian lore. Without a doubt, he was being tested. He wanted to have as much information as he could muster at his fingertips. His and Zoe's lives might well depend upon nothing more than his ability to recall those legends he had deposited in his memory bank.

Due to his own most recent experiences, Sham decided to concentrate his efforts of recollection on the North American Hopi. The old apparition who had confronted him before his encounter with the snakes was dressed in the manner of an Anasazi, generally considered to be the ancestors of the Hopi.

He had been relating a Hopi story of the creation to Zoe when this expedition first began, and he had recently survived two ordeals by using a Hopi magic water jar, which legend asserts, was given to the clans by the guardian spirit of the Fourth World. He focused his efforts of recollection on that legend.

When planted in the ground, the jar would bring water to arid land. One person of purity was appointed to carry the jar and plant it anew at each stop along their migrations. If the jar was broken a special ritual was necessary to replace it. At the moment, the full details of the ritual slipped his mind, but he knew that he could not do it alone.

CHAPTER XV

Anasazi

Shaman continued along the now brighter pathway, his thoughts engaged by stories of the Hopi migrations. These had been recorded across the continent on cave walls, ancient rocks, desert sands, and even as a great mound of earth in the shape of a snake left on an Ohio prairie centuries ago.

Many histories of the different clans paraded across the field of his memory. They were too numerous to count, but each had left an indelible footprint. Sham was pleased to know that he could recall so much of the long unused information. He felt fortified for whatever might lie ahead. His own arduous journey was beginning to resemble the great migrations.

Shaman soon came upon a burial cave that held the remains of several human skeletons, including one of a child. He picked up the small skull and carried it some distance as he studied it more closely.

The back of the skull was fragmented, and several other fractures were evident over the eye sockets and the right temple. Shaman theorized that the child had probably died as a result of a fall from a cliff dwelling. During the fall, the little head had probably come into contact with numerous rocks projecting from the cliff.

It could have been no simple feat for a parent with a child to climb precarious ladders accessing those remote caves. And one would have to be very vigilant to insure the safety of any youngsters left behind when the people worked their fields.

Amongst the ruins it was not uncommon to find rooms with only one small opening too high for a child to reach. The little skull was a poignant example to nurture Shaman's theory that some thoughtful architect of the past had insisted on the height of this portal as a precautionary measure to improve the Anasazi equivalent of the nursery. As he silently applauded the imaginary architect, Sham heard an eerie, muffled cry.

He listened intently, but heard nothing more. He returned to scrutinizing the skull and, once again, heard the pitiful cries. This time it sounded so much like a lost child that Sham was determined to search the area. He put the little skull on a boulder and rushed back along the trail, but discovered no evidence of anyone in the immediate vicinity.

The cries of mischievous zephyrs can be really unsettling. I mustn't be spooked like some schoolboy, he cautioned himself.

He walked back toward the cave. Now the cries were definitely emanating from behind him. He returned to where the skull of the Anasazi child lay forlornly on the large rock. He remembered how hard he and Rachel had worked to help Native Americans reclaim the remains of their ancestors whose bones had ended up on dusty basement shelves in museums. He quickly returned the tiny cranium to its resting place beside the remainder of its Anasazi family. He heard no more of the mournful sounds as the present terrain began to demand a great deal from his tired muscles.

He soon came upon a deserted village of about a dozen rooms tucked beneath a low natural overhang. Shaman sat down to rest in the middle of the little village plaza. The uphill climb had taken its toll on his dwindling energy. He dozed off, only to awake a few moments later in the company of four elderly Indians. While he slept, they had arranged themselves in a small circle, he included in it.

The one who first stood to speak was undeniably the leader of the group. He wore an impressive necklace of bear claws, and his well-muscled body stood a foot taller than the other three. Sham imagined that the bear, whose claws the giant wore, had probably never known what hit it.

The voice that emanated from the massive chest, while the bear claw necklace rose and fell with each breath, had a deep resonance that demanded one's attention. Shaman could understand the speaker perfectly. He did not know how, for the man spoke no dialect with which Sham was familiar.

"You have been tested twice and found true," the deep voice erupted from behind the bear claws. "This is a holy place. Here you may rest and learn. Then you will be allowed to return to the Fourth World with our words." After this pronouncement, the elders began, one at a time, to speak of man's transgressions.

"Man has forgotten that he is a spiritual being," said the first.

"He has abandoned the teachings that all things are entwined and that he has a duty to the universe," added the second.

"Just as the animal he eats, the stars above, the air he breathes, or the rocks beneath his feet, man has a place in the cosmic harmony," said the third. The last elder in the circle prophesied.

"If man continues to live by the laws of greed, the Fourth World will be destroyed. Only those who respect their Creator and live in harmony with nature will be allowed to enter the Fifth World.

"Since you have remembered the ways of your ancestors, and you have passed the test of courage, you will join us on our voyage to the realm of universal knowledge. When you return, you will understand the task for which you are needed," the leader spoke once more. *Universal knowledge? The collective consciousness?*

Shaman was excited by the possibility. He often hypothesized that sporadic occurrences of extra-sensory perception and apparitional sightings might stem from nothing more than a psychic ability that all people were born with, but most had forgotten how to use.

He and Rachel had often tried to tap this psychic fountain. A few times they had been at least nominally successful in crossing that invisible line that separates the physical reality from the metaphysical and individual will from a cosmic predilection. Sham's most vivid memory of such an occasion was the Ya Ya ceremony when men and animals seemed to become interchangeable. As Sham's thoughts dwelled on the Ya Ya, one of the elders was drawing a circle of cornmeal. When the perimeter was complete, he invited Shaman to enter. As Sham entered the circle, he heard the rhythmic beat of a distant drum. He saw a stone fetish, surrounded by pahos, sitting on an altar in the center of the circle.

Another of the elders emptied the remaining cornmeal from its horn container into a shallow bowl beneath the fetish. The elder added to this, from yet another horn, a sticky white substance that reminded Shaman of the poison liquid that bleeds from an oleander bush when it is trimmed.

The elder drank from the bowl and passed it next to Clawing Bear (the name Sham had silently given to the large Indian). Clawing Bear sipped from the bowl before passing it on to Shaman.

"This is the milk of the Earth. Drink to feed your spirit." Sham managed to quell his fear and drank a mouthful of the musky potion that reminded him of a mother's breast milk, before passing it to the next elder in the circle.

Four times the bowl was passed. After each drink, he had more difficulty focusing. Soon, the elders receded to a far distance. The sound of silence engulfed Shaman, turning his thoughts inward. He relived the moment of his birth and beyond, floating in the absolute security of his mother's womb, before he was abruptly catapulted back to the ceremonial circle, the elders once again at his side.

Then a cornhusk filled with a tobacco-like substance was lit and passed around the circle. Each participant puffed once, twice, thrice, and finally, a fourth time while fanning the exhaled smoke back over his face. Shaman was getting very light-headed. He could actually feel his temperature rising. He had not smoked for many years, but the substance he had just inhaled did not remind him of any commercial tobaccos that had been prevalent in his youth. Certainly none had ever made his blood begin to boil as it coursed through his veins.

Following this ritual smoking, each of the elders placed another prayer feather among the other pahos. They turned to Shaman, patiently waiting for him to do the same. Shaman had no prepared paho. Then he remembered the eagle feather that he had retrieved from the magic water jar. He placed this beside the other pahos on the altar. Shaman's paho was not so beautifully assembled as were the others with a small portion of cornmeal wrapped in husks and attached with twined cotton—but his would do as well. It had been truly earned.

The circle of elders began an intricate chant. Shaman sang along. The syllables of this ceremonial song were as familiar as his name and rolled from his tongue effortlessly. With each new tone Shaman's spirit soared higher. They continued to chant, ceasing only long enough to again partake of the milk of Earth and to smoke the strange cigarette until the present lost its hold.

As though looking through a telescope, Sham saw himself as a tiny ant sitting in a pinpoint of light, surrounded by a timeless void. Suddenly he felt himself explode into an infinite universe of particles of light. There was oneness, all-inclusive, each particle belonging to the whole. He was the Creator and that which had been created.

He experienced life in all its evolutionary forms; from its conception in primordial ooze until its present and future mutations. He was animate and inanimate, animal and man, stone and star. He was the power of good and the power of evil. Sham's heartbeat became the rhythmic beat of the Ya Ya, and his breathing resonated the deep Huh, Huh of a large animal. He reveled in the glory of creation. Then his breath became a gasp, a strangled cry for oxygen. He was nature's plan which had become distorted. He was drowning in the cataclysmic results of humanity's unharnessed greed.

When Shaman thought he could not avoid suffocation, he felt another presence, a warm, soft, comforting presence. His breathing eased. He was content beyond earthly contentment. He was whole. He was love. Shaman instinctively reached out to Rachel. When he opened his eyes, he was alone. The old ruin had disappeared. There were no elders, no altar, no sign that anything had happened—except for his eagle feather which was lying where the center of the circle would have been. Next to it was the wingtip of an eagle.

He knew now what he had been chosen for. The ancient Ya Ya ritual, meant to unite man with his animal brothers and ensure each his rightful place in the harmony of nature, had been perverted into the practice of magic for purposes of greed. The leader of the ceremony was not a priest following the ageless recipe that would benefit all humans and animals, but a two-heart whose only purpose was personal gain.

Through the misuse of the Ya Ya ritual, the two-heart had released humanity's lust to consume and control, and nature's scales were out of balance. It would be Shaman's task to expose the witch who had subverted the force of the ancient ritual. Nature's harmony could not be restored until the power of the Ya Ya was returned to its original intent. Shaman was struck dumb by the magnitude of the task which had been set for him.

He had experienced the collective consciousness and made contact with Rachel on that higher plane. She had brought him breath when he could not breathe. She had strengthened him with love when he was almost lost. He thought of her with longing. He saw her sitting in her pottery shed, her fingers molding wet clay into a thing of beauty, her mind attuned to a different place but her hands never faltering.

He did not doubt that they had briefly touched in that realm of meditation. Rachel had joined him on his journey, and they were love. Holding this comfort to his heart, Shaman collected the feather and the wingtip and resumed his climb. He quickly arrived at another fork in the path. To his left, as before, he could see a narrow tunnel; to the right, an open plain.

This time Shaman never hesitated. He had learned his lesson. The easy path had not shortened his journey. He noticed a faint trail of cornmeal as he entered the narrow opening. He retrieved a little of the cornmeal and put it in his pocket before continuing along this arterial pathway through the body of Mother Earth.

CHAPTER XVI

Rachel waited nervously for Clyde to call. She had read this same page twice already. Her mind refused to focus on the legend of the twins who had to be sacrificed to the great red-bellied snake in order to save the people from destruction.

She started the first paragraph once more. Before she had read two lines, the printed words dissolved in undulating waves, replaced by an image of Shaman being menaced by a huge snake. Sham's only weapon was a stone water jar.

Rachel had never known such terror. She watched as Shaman bravely wrestled the snake's head into the jar and then danced his escape through a strange tunnel door. Mentally she rushed to where he sat with his forehead on his crossed arms.

As though starved for the sight of her, Shaman touched her face and body. Hiding her fear, she teasingly called him a dirty old man. Then she cradled his head in her lap. He was so still that she thought he might have been bitten. Then his breathing returned to normal. He was only tired and frightened.

Rachel shut the book with a start. She was shaken by the intensity of the vision. Shaman was in a place she did not recognize, and he was in great danger. Why had Zoe not been with him? Surely he would never voluntarily be parted from her.

During times of stress Rachel often went to her pottery studio, and she did so now. While working with her hands in the smooth, wet clay, she pictured the water jar that she had seen Shaman using to tame the huge, red-bellied snake. The jar had not been shaped like the typical water container. This one had a pointed bottom, and it was embellished with an unusual design. While her hands worked steadily to form a clay replica of the water jar in her vision, Rachel let her mind surrender to a state of meditation.

Rachel opened her eyes, rising slowly from that place of tranquility. She checked the large clock on the cedar wall of her workroom. Lengthening shadows crept across the old bay window seat, confirming that she had not been in the present world for much longer than her usual twenty minute meditation. The air around her smelled of the scent of fresh flowers, but her mouth was as dry as dust.

She drank a glass of cool water and brought the water pitcher back to the worktable. There, she found a fully shaped water jar with a pointed bottom. It was as though her hands knew the pattern and required nothing of her but her physical presence. The jar lacked only the design that would render it identical to the one she had seen in her recent vision.

She felt an urgency to complete the jar and quickly added the design to ready it for the kiln. Beginning at the bottom of the container, she painted a star-burst, expanding upward to the narrow neck. Around the neck she painted four circles, red, yellow, white, and black. Rachel studied the finished jar closely. The star-like pattern was like none she could recall.

While she contemplated this new-born universe, Rachel had an intense memory of being with Shaman, and they were part of this very creation exploding throughout a limitless space.

Rachel knew that she had a role in whatever was to come, and her replication of the water jar was a necessary part of that role. Whatever force was guiding her would direct her movements as surely as a written script. She must follow her instincts without question.

Just in case a part of the unknown plan might require some desert trekking, Rachel changed into heavier clothes. She did not relish the thought of rushing to the top of some precarious mesa without the proper protective clothing. Good high-topped hiking shoes were a must. While fiber sandals or hide moccasins may have sufficed for ancient Indians, she had no intentions of trusting her feet and ankles to the mercies of snakes, cactus quills or rough terrain.

She put on a woolen blouse and slacks. The soft wool would be better protection than cotton if it should rain. She chose a practical straw hat and added a light scarf. She laid out her wind-breaker and checked the batteries in the large flashlight. It wasn't disposable like the newer lights, and it was getting harder and harder to procure batteries, but she trusted it. Over the years, it had been a godsend.

She took a few moments to go through her mental checklist; water, light, protective clothing. Her own four-wheel drive was in good repair and boasted the usual spare tire and two extra fuel batteries. Warm sleeping bags and a medical kit were stored within its muddled interior.

As she stashed the flashlight inside her backpack, she let her mind dwell on the strange circumstances of how she had come into possession of this particular light. She recalled that it had been just before the turn of the twenty-first century. Like a video replaying in her head, Rachel relived the memory as though it were happening now.

Rachel and Shaman loaded their traveling gear as they prepared to set out to study the cave ruins at Betatakin. In its gaping, red sandstone mouth, arched palate rising over two hundred feet, this great cave had once sheltered a large Anasazi village. They planned to continue on to Keet Seel, an even larger cave village about ten miles from Betatakin. It was known to the Hopi as Talastima, but the Navaho term, meaning "broken pottery," was the one most often used in popular vernacular.

Keet Seel could only be approached on foot or horseback, so before entering the canyon, they made arrangements to pick up two horses from a nearby rancher. At the ranch Shaman went to the corral to pick out two good-natured animals. Rachel was relaxing on the shaded porch when a woman with startling green eyes approached from around the corner.

"I think you could use this, my dear," said the stranger, extending a large, old-fashioned light toward Rachel.

"Thank you so much, but I packed a new one," Rachel politely refused.

"We had better get going, Rachel," she heard Shaman call, and she turned toward his voice.

"Coming," she responded. When she turned back to say goodbye to the pleasant stranger, the woman had gone.

Rachel joined Shaman and began stowing items into the saddlebags. Before adding her new flashlight, she pressed the switch. Nothing; she replaced the batteries and tried again; again, nothing. They couldn't continue without a flashlight. A desert ruin is no place to be stumbling around in after dark.

Shaman offered to buy a light from the rancher. He refused their money but made a gift of one that looked like the same implement the strange woman had offered to Rachel.

"While I was waiting on your porch, a very nice lady just offered this same light to me," Rachel told the rancher. "Will you tell her that this time I am very pleased to accept?"

"I don't know who it could have been," replied the rancher. "The Missus is shopping today. I'm fending for myself 'til she gets back." Rachel did not dwell on the incident for very long as she let herself become immersed in the sights and sounds of the gnarled pinòn pine and blue-berried juniper forest on the canyon rim. The musky smell of sage was everywhere. She watched a turkey buzzard glide toward its prey, while a small scrub jay sang from a gnarled branch of pine.

As she followed the trail between the grotesquely shaped pines and junipers, Rachel felt as if she were riding through some primeval forest. They picked their way down the precarious trail and approached the cave from the canyon floor. Here, the brush and quaking aspen encroached upon the deserted village itself. Unlike the sparser vegetation and deformed forest of the mesa, the canyon supported a growth that was almost tropical in its denseness.

The yawning mouth of the Great Cave gaped wide in the sheer cliff rising hundreds of feet above. Rachel wondered if the sound of a symphony playing in this naturally curved amphitheater would be magnificent. She listened for the timbre of long-silent drums that might still be reverberating in the nooks and crannies of the domed aperture. There was only silence, but she smiled at the possibility of a hidden note finding its way to the ear of an unsuspecting audience.

Although they had explored Betatakin before, the marvelous ruins still filled her with a sense of awe. Rachel looked at the many rooms that had been neatly sealed, and felt a wave of expectation, as though the occupants might be returning at any time.

After three days in Betatakin, Rachel and Shaman were ready to move on to Keet Seel. After dinner, Rachel handed the sand-scrubbed cooking utensils to Shaman. "While you're packing up, I think I'll try to get a few sketches of that pictograph I discovered this morning."

"You'd better hurry, then," Shaman called over his shoulder as he added the pots to the gear being readied for their departure at daybreak.

Although dusk came early to the gloomy canyon floor, she thought she would have enough time before dark to do a few sketches and make it back to camp. She took the old flashlight and started out on her own.

About a fifteen minute hike down the box canyon, Rachel ducked inside a narrow break in the seemingly solid sandstone wall and followed the little trail that led back into the canyon cliff, where she had noticed some markings. Taking her sketch pad, she hurried to catch the last of the day's light. The trail ended where Rachel found the paintings. She leaned against a protruding boulder to balance her pad and began to sketch. The boulder shifted, sending Rachel tumbling down a hidden entrance to an undiscovered cave network.

She tried to climb back up, but the entrance was ten feet above her head and offered no footholds. Shaman was too far up the canyon to hear her cries. Hoping to find a trail through the caves that would connect to the Great Cave, Rachel groped her way deeper into the subterranean room and tried to chase away her fear.

Betatakin was inhabited during the period of the long drought. Perhaps these rooms held the meager stores which the inhabitants could forage until they finally had to abandon the settlement for lack of game in the area. The caves could also have been used as burial chambers. Rachel quickly chose to think of them as storage rooms.

She used the flashlight sparingly to get her bearings. There was no time to waste investigating the caverns. Staying to her left, hoping to avoid a passage that might lead her only deeper into the mountain, she moved uphill. She entered and exited several fair sized rooms before she had to use the flashlight to continue. A few moments later, Rachel emerged into the middle of a large ceremonial kiva.

She had seen many of these subterranean rooms where the Anasazi conducted their religious rituals, but this was the first one that had ever raised the hair on the nape of her neck. Maybe it was just the surprise of finding a hidden kiva. After all, they were usually dug in the midst of the villages, within easy access of the residents.

The expected ladder leading to a hole in the surface was missing, but a series of small slits that could be used as hand holds had been carved into the side of the wall.

Rachel tied her flashlight to her belt and began to scale the wall. When she arrived at the opening, it was night. She looked back at the surrounding rocks and brush. Even with the light of a full moon, she could barely find the kiva entrance. She heard Shaman calling her name. After marking the entrance, she called back and flashed her light so he could see her coming. The kiva opening was just a short distance from the Great Cave, but it was perfectly camouflaged.

Shaman grabbed her arm and spun her tightly against his chest, wrapping his other arm around her. She felt the panic in his touch as her body molded itself to him. "Thank God you're safe! When you hadn't returned by dark, I was frantic. I found the trail to the markings and thought you might have twisted an ankle. When you were nowhere in sight, I thought of mountain lions and other wild creatures that still roam these canyons. Old prospectors have left mine fields of open shafts for the unwary hiker." His face, illuminated by the light of the crude torch he had used to light his search area changed swiftly from panic to relief, to passion.

Their lovemaking was heightened by the fear that had sparked it. No touch was close enough, no thrust deep enough to erase the terror of losing one another as they made love until dawn. In the morning, Shaman followed her down the small kiva opening.

"Do you feel the oppressiveness, Shaman? The air is almost tangibly heavy. It gives me a terrible sense of foreboding."

"It certainly doesn't emit the sanctified feeling of a chapel," Sham replied. They looked at the symbols of horned animals staring back at them from the cave walls and took note of the central fire pit.

"That pit is as large as the one used during the Ya Ya," Rachel remarked. "Maybe the Old Ones held that ceremony here. I still marvel at the feats performed by those dancers in Chaco Canyon. Especially when some of them rolled in the hot coals of the fire without suffering burns."

"I know," Shaman agreed. "To this day, I'm not sure that the dancers weren't actually transformed into animals. That's as close as we'll ever come to pure magic. Perhaps you've stumbled upon some secret society's ceremonial kiva, Rachel?"

The malignant atmosphere prompted them to take only a cursory inventory of the room's contents. The need to start their journey to Keet Seel was all the excuse they needed to leave without exploring any of the other caverns.

The clock struck the hour, bringing Rachel's thoughts back to the present. She once more touched the old flashlight and looked at the timepiece. Why hadn't Clyde called?

It would take only five minutes to drive to the airstrip. She hoped the runway was in good enough condition for a landing. She had sent one of the ranch hands to do some maintenance on it a few weeks ago, just in case Clyde might decide to drop in for a visit.

Rachel paced across the floor a few times before sitting down to meditate. She let her mind reach out to Zoe.

CHAPTER XVII

Lessons

As Clyde split the blackness with his super-jet, he thought of the Arizona of his youth. He remembered his father taking him out into the desert brush, not far from the orchards and fields of the Thomas ranch. His father's voice echoed in the cockpit.

"Remember, son, water always runs downhill. These washes are its highways. Sometimes a low spot can yield water if you dig beneath the sand. Look for the places where there's some vegetation surviving, or dig on the outside edge of a sharp bend." Clyde imagined his father's face reflected in the blackness of the windshield as he continued his instructions.

"Don't eat any part of that plant with the bluish green leaves and white bugle flowers. That's datura. It's poison and can cause hallucinations. You can eat most dark berries, but avoid the white and yellow and red ones, unless you know they are edible. If they're formed like a raspberry, you can probably eat them."

Clyde had listened closely to his father and learned to read tracks, how to follow a wash to water, what plants were full of moisture and which were medicinal. He shared all this acquired expertise with his blood-brother. From mountain forests to the painted-desert, Shaman and Clyde skied the snowy slopes and shared the mysteries of ancient desert ruins. As young men, they covered most of the Navaho Nation on horseback. Each rode bareback as well as any brave, and they spent countless nights camping out on Arizona's diversified terrain.

Now his father's reflection was replaced by the memory of that long ride after the death of Shaman's parents. Clyde had never shed tears easily, but on that ride they had flowed freely as the two young men rode their horses to lather. He felt Shaman's pain and guilt that he could do nothing to help. He grieved for two people who had never been anything but kind to Clyde.

Clyde attended the ceremony on that fateful night. The police had questioned him briefly. No one could really think he would ever hurt a member of Shaman's family. He and Shaman were like brothers.

Clyde's thoughts turned to his own family and scenes of the little farm in Canyon de Chelly, which his mother had always referred to as Koyongtupqa, (canyon of the wild turkeys.)

From the age of ten, until they had gone away to college, Clyde and Shaman spent their summers in the mud hogan and tended the crops on his father's small tract. Weekends, Clyde's family would join them, and while his parents sold jewelry and rugs to the tourists, his sisters played in the waters of the receding stream bed.

Summer always seemed too little time to farm and hunt and share their dreams. Hidden behind the tall stand of tamarisks and Russian olives that were strangling out the few remaining cottonwoods, they heard the tourists being driven through the center of the canyon in their noisy, open transports, but the foliage was so thick that the sightseers could spy no more than the smoke from Clyde's fire.

As his jet ate up the miles of sky, Clyde pictured the empty ruins peering out from their caves and crevices, and he could hear the canyon walls echoing the cries and laughter of the Navaho people. He felt the presence of the Hisatsinom spirits who had watched him from those ruins. He did not think of them as Anasazi, (ancient enemy.) They were the forebears of his mother's people.

As a child, using the old handholds hewn into the canyon walls by his mother's predecessors, he'd climbed to the deserted cave dwellings and performed his prayer rituals in an ancient kiva high above the canyon floor. From this vantage point he looked down upon the Navaho inhabitants who were his father's people, and he felt the power of being both old and new.

He wondered if some of his own ancestors might have built one of the twelfth century ruins tucked into the canyon walls, only to be driven out by a faction of his own Navaho forefathers. He fervently hoped that his Navaho ancestors had not been the cause of the demise of the Hisatsinom.

Chapter XVIII

Sacrifice

While Clyde raced toward Rachel, Zoe was enjoying an ancient legend being recounted by a storyteller.

"The people were instructed to travel to the four corners of the world and to live in peace and to remember to be thankful," the narrator was saying.

Zoe had heard her grandfather recount this same story. According to the legend, man did pretty well for a while, but just couldn't get the part about peace right. So the Creator picked a few good people to start over with. Before destroying the world, He sent those people to live with the ants beneath the Earth. The people stayed with the ants until the world could be rebuilt. That, supposedly, is why ants have such small waists. They had to share their food with the people and, because they were of a generous nature, had to keep tightening their own belts.

In these stories, animals could talk, just like the deer who offered itself for dinner. Men could see in the dark as well as any animal, but man's inner eye had to be nourished with the knowledge and practice of harmony or sight was lost.

There were also wise spirits who would guide the people and help them take care of one another. Some of these spirits were said to come from other planets and stars, and some represented plants and animals and long-dead ancestors.

Zoe loved these legends because she knew they were more than mere stories. These were the religious history of ancient men. The children sat out in the sunshine in a circle around the storyteller and relived the adventures of man since the beginning of time.

In the center of the circle a large swastika was drawn on the ground. Zoe's grandfather had taught her that to the Hisatsinom this symbol represented man's migrations to the four corners of the earth. It had nothing to do with the World War II emblem. Here, the sign was beautiful. Hitler had stolen the symbol and made it ugly in infamy.

In this place, people knew the importance of animals. Elsewhere, she had seen geese with their feet nailed to the floor. In this village, people praised nature and took only what they needed to live. She had breathed the air of a different world and had seen the belching bellies of waste disposals consuming the refuse of unleashed greed.

In her heart, Zoe knew that people could have it all. They needed to respect the Earth. They should remember their place in the world. Most of all, they needed to heal the damage already done.

Since Alo had brought Zoe to this village no one had questioned her right to be here, nor treated her any differently from the other children. She was free to roam the flowery meadows and climb the giant trees. She played with the animals and raced with the other young ones. This was her time of learning what the world could be like, what it once was. It was her time to choose life.

Just as the storyteller finished his tale, Zoe felt the Earth begin to tremble. Soon even the great trees were swaying back and forth, their roots straining to keep their trunks anchored to the ground. The people who were gathered in the village center milled about in confusion. Then the Earth began to toss them helter-skelter.

Zoe saw some of the people tying themselves to the strips of rawhide that festooned the large trees nearby. Her young hunting companion came running into the village. He shouted a warning that the great red-bellied water snake had risen in the nearby lake and was demanding a sacrifice. The parents began clutching their children to their breasts. None wanted their sons or daughters to be chosen as the sacrifice.

Zoe remembered Alo's words, "You have been well chosen," and knew that her previous fears had finally been realized. When the young hunter pointed to Zoe, there could be no doubt. He nervously informed the elders that it was Zoe whom the snake had demanded as the sacrifice.

This caused quite a quandary amongst the elders. Zoe was not theirs to offer. Only she could decide if she would ransom the village as demanded. Her knees were shaking, not from the quaking of the Earth, but from sheer terror. She knew she could run away but, if she did, the village would be forfeited. No one suggested that she must save them. The choice was hers alone. The people waited for her decision.

Zoe thought of her family and wanted desperately to find herself waking from a bad dream, back in her own room, but she did not awaken. The ground continued to quake beneath her feet. She looked at all her newly acquired friends who had demonstrated harmony and selflessness in the way they chose to live, and she knew that she must meet the ransom.

Before she could change her mind Zoe ran quickly toward the little lake. The people trailed behind her. When she finally saw the great snake, she did not think she could go through with it. The snake rose from the water. It looked even more terrifying than she had imagined. It swayed its giant head, and the Earth shook more violently.

Zoe closed her eyes and crept to the edge of the water. She took another step and felt the water rise above her ankles. She squeezed her eyes even more tightly shut. The huge snake lunged, wrapped itself around her, and plunged beneath the lake.

The Earth ceased its quaking, and the people returned to their village. As they untied their rawhide harnesses, they sang their thanks to the little stranger who had cared more for them and their world than for herself. She would not be forgotten as long as stories could be told.

Zoe felt the snake wrapping itself around her. She took a deep breath and prayed that whatever happened would be over with quickly. As she was plunged beneath the water she thought of flowers and sunshine and berries.

Her chest burned, and she began to lose consciousness. Just as her lungs were emptied of air, she found herself gasping for breath, lying on dry land. She was in a large underground cave, and a river was rushing behind her. Alo was standing nearby. The snake was nowhere in sight.

"You are very brave, Zoe," said Alo. "The time has come for you to return to your grandfather. Follow the caverns directly ahead. There you will find a ladder leading to the surface."

Zoe couldn't believe her ears. She ran to throw her arms around Alo. She looked up into the guide's face and stared into warm, loving, turquoise eyes.

"Will I ever see you again?" Zoe asked.

"From time to time the occasion might arise," answered Alo. "Go now and give my love to Shaman."

With these final words, Alo disappeared, and Zoe stepped quickly into the next empty cavern. She followed a circuitous route through several caves until she finally saw the ladder directly ahead. Before she could reach it, Shaman came walking through another opening. Zoe ran to him as fast as her legs would carry her.

CHAPTER XIX

Reunion

In a deep trance, Rachel could feel her granddaughter reaching out to her in fear. There appeared a fleeting vision of the cold snake-eyes of the ugly reptile that had so recently menaced Shaman. Then, just as briefly, that vision was replaced by another of eyes the shade of turquoise and warm as a summer day. She recognized these eyes. They belonged to the woman who had offered the old flashlight to her.

Rachel imagined a kiva ladder sticking out of the ground, and she felt the presence of Shaman and Zoe. Another visionary flash of pottery shards told her where she would find them. They were together beneath the ruins of Keet Seel.

At least now she had a destination. She never doubted for a moment that she knew their location. Clyde should be here soon, but she didn't dare wait for him. Her gear, along with the newly fashioned water jar, was already in the jeep. She sent Pappy to the airstrip with a note to tell Clyde her destination and ask him to come as quickly as he could.

Rachel took all the shortcuts she could remember. Spraying cinders in a wide arc, the four-wheeler roared up Devil Dog Road. By the time she merged with the traffic on I-40, Rachel had the vehicle at its maximum speed. She had made the distance in a matter of minutes and raced toward the turnoff to Highway 160. She covered the sixty miles to Tuba City in record time.

Another five minutes and she was past the entrance to the dinosaur tracks, 200 million year old footprints that had been left on a prehistoric mud flat to mark the passage of those long-extinct giants. Over time, the mud flat had turned to rock more solid than concrete, preserving the prints of these ancient beasts. Tonight they meant only that she was a few miles closer to Keet Seel.

She had another fifty miles to hurtle toward the turnoff to Route 564. Ten more miles, and she would have to abandon the jeep.

Rachel had been in such a hurry that she had not thought to call ahead to arrange for a horse—one of the few species of animal that had managed, in modest numbers, to adapt to today's world. But forgotten she had, and she wasn't going to waste any time worrying about it. She still possessed two good feet.

Strapping the water jar to her back-pack, Rachel grabbed the trusty old flashlight and attacked the trail at a dead-run.

Thank God I've been to these old ruins often enough to find them in the dark. She stumbled in haste over rocks and rabbit brush, cuts and bruises going unnoticed in her race to reach the people she loved most in the world.

As Rachel dashed madly toward Keet Seel, Shaman and Zoe approached the ladder that would finally release them from this subterranean maze. Suddenly, a pudding thick fog enveloped them, and a disembodied voice spoke from the invisible reaches of the cavern. Shaman thought he recognized the voice as that of Clawing Bear.

"Remember Kawestima," (Betakin) said the voice. "Rest here at Talastima for a while, Shaman. You must purify yourself and restore the magic water jar. Both of you must armor yourselves against evil." The voice ceased, and the fog rolled away. As the last wispy tendrils of the ghostly fog receded, Shaman heard another voice.

"Hold my hand," came the soft echo, "and we'll walk together." He knew this voice, too. Once again, his mother had come to comfort him. She took his hand and guided them to the ladder. Shaman and Zoe climbed its rungs and emerged in the prehistoric cliff dwelling of Talastima (Keet Seel).

Over the period of his lifetime, the old pueblo village had become familiar to him. Tucked beneath a gaping wound in the side of a towering cliff, these ruins had withstood the ravages of time for nearly a thousand years of wind, sun, pot-seekers, archaeologists and tourists. But tonight, there were none of these.

The only presence Shaman could discern were the Hisatsinom spirits of the original settlers of this remote civilization. He could see them fashioning their pottery, curing hides, designing their pahos with loving care, and offering thanks to their guiding spirits.

Shaman took Zoe to a sheltered room, cradled her with his body and stroked her cheek. If his road to this place had been a trial, he could only imagine what the trip must have cost his granddaughter.

"We'll talk later, Zoe. Now you need some rest." Zoe slept in her grandfather's arms. She dreamed sporadically of flowery vistas and great red-bellied snakes. When she tossed in fright, Shaman soothed her back to a peaceful sleep.

Sham contemplated Clawing Bear's last remarks echoing from the spirit fog. "Remember Kawestima," he had said, using the Hopi name for Betatakin. Sham combed his memory for any information that might be of value concerning the nearby ruin.

And what about the rest of Clawing Bear's remarks: How was he to restore the magic water jar? This would be another challenge to research in the dusty references of his mental library. Like a computer in overdrive, Shaman's brain sorted through the information stored there.

The purification process alone will require four days of fasting and meditation. Will we have to remain in this desolate place for another four days? And what of food and water for Zoe? There hasn't been a water supply available to Keet Seel in years. Maybe we should go to Betatakin now?

As these thoughts raced through his mind, Shaman heard a noise. Someone—or something—was stumbling through the ruins. At this point, he would not have been surprised at any apparition that might wander into their humble shelter. The noise grew nearer. He braced himself and cradled Zoe more tightly to his body.

Before he could see her, he heard his name from Rachel's sweet lips and called to her with joy. Rachel flew into the darkened room and threw herself across them. Shaman found her tears of relief more refreshing than the pure crystal water from the magic water jar. He had to touch her over and over to be sure that she was real. He had thought of her so often during this amazing journey that he feared she might only be another figment of his imagination.

Zoe wakened and clutched Rachel tightly. No one spoke. There was too much to be told, and none of them knew where to begin. Each held the others and cried for joy.

CHAPTER XX

The Ya Ya

Now it was Clyde's Hopi grandfather who stared at him from the cockpit window. The old man's voice filled Clyde's head.

"The Old Ones who came before were farmers and had no will for killing." These Hisatsinom, according to his grandfather, were a peaceable tribe who extended their friendship and help to all who approached them. They were no fair match for marauding tribes bent on violence. In his Hopi grandfather's stories, the Tavasuh, the Navaho's ancestors, were thieves and head-pounders. They had few redeeming qualities and no stories to tell by the winter fires.

"You must remember to respect the old ways. Your father is Navaho, but you are Hopi. The Navaho have learned much from our ancestors, but there is still a lot they do not know. If you choose to follow the ways of the Hopi, these things I will teach you."

Clyde heard his grandfather as clearly as he had heard those words at the age of six. The year it was decided into which of the Hopi societies Clyde would be initiated. This was the only subject which Clyde could remember hearing his parents argue about, and it remained a sore spot with his father for many years.

In a quarrelsome tone, his father would say to his mother, "Your clan is important in the tribe. Your son should be initiated into the Powamu society. Why is he being brought into the Kachina society instead? Do you think a priest will come from the Kachinas? How will he ever be respected as a leader of the clan's ceremony?"

"It is of no real importance," Clyde's mother would answer. "He will still participate in the power of the clan. That is what is important." To her, the argument was finished.

Over the years, Clyde's grandfather taught him many Hopi rituals. I always felt a little guilty whenever I performed grandfather's ceremonies in the Navaho hogan in Canyon de Chelly, Clyde admitted to himself. The windowless hogan was constructed aboveground, but it was not dissimilar to the Hopi kiva. It had a dirt floor and center fire pit but was entered by a door, rather than a hole in the roof. The walls held a few pegs for garments and shelves for other necessities. The only other furniture was a small table and his bedroll.

He knew the traditional stories of both the Hopi and Navaho tribes and recognized similarities in much of their lore. They often took each other in for protection from one enemy or another and shared many customs and habits. They had also, over the years, had many occasions to be enemies.

Land disputes were usually at the heart of his grandfather's interpretations of their disagreements, as in the late 1800s, when the Hopi had found themselves suddenly relegated to a small reservation completely surrounded by the Navaho Nation. As the Navaho increased their numbers and became more Americanized in nature, the Hopi became more reclusive and sectarian.

The old ways were dying out in both cultures. As fewer of the young people were willing to learn the rituals of their grandparents, Clyde became the repository for the ancient lore recounted by both his Navaho father and his Hopi grandfather, and he understood its power.

"You are not only Hopi." Clyde's father's voice broke into his thoughts. "You are also my son, and you must learn the Navaho Way. You have learned much from the White Man, as well. The time is long past when we could remain isolated from their influence. It is up to you to decide how much they can take from you and how much you will take from them." Clyde remembered how his father had urged him to ask his Hopi grandfather to teach Clyde the ritual of the Ya Ya.

"He is one of the few men living who can give you that knowledge. It is a very powerful ceremony," Clyde heard his own twelve-year-old voice ask.

"Does anyone still practice the Ya Ya?"

"Most people think it has been extinct for some years, but I have heard that a few still practice it," his father answered. "Your grandfather has the knowledge of the Ya Ya. He can teach you its secrets. You must ask him to allow you to carry this knowledge for the future."

In spite of his father's frequent urgings, Clyde did not approach his grandfather with this request. But when Clyde turned thirteen, he had a vision. In this vision, there were no animals left on the Earth, and men were looking everywhere for one who had the power to recall them. The people turned to Clyde and asked him to tell them his grandfather's secret. But he had not known the secret, and the people had left with shuffling feet and bowed heads, asking themselves how they would be able to survive with no animal brothers. The following day, Clyde asked his grandfather to teach him the Ya Ya.

"That is too much power for you, little one," his grandfather refused.

"I am no longer little," Clyde had answered. "Teach me slowly as I grow. You will be the one to judge my readiness. You can teach me all but some small portion of the ritual that is necessary. When your time becomes short, you will be able to teach me the rest quickly," Clyde implored reasonably.

He convinced his grandfather that he would be a patient student. And, indeed, he was. Clyde was twenty-three when the last of the knowledge of the Ya Ya ceremony was imparted to him. His grandfather guarded the final instructions until the bitter end. At death's door, he called Clyde to him and sent everyone else away before he entrusted the last of the ceremonial liturgy to his favorite grandson.

"Finally," said Clyde's father from the cockpit window. "Now you will always be respected by the clan." Clyde was happy that his father's spirit was pleased. It was an honor to hold the knowledge imparted by his grandfather, but at the time, Clyde had not known anyone who was anxious to have him perform the ceremony.

He recalled the first time he attempted to practice the newly learned ritual. His father had accompanied him to a secluded cave near the ranch. The full ceremony had not been completed when they had heard someone nearby, and Clyde stopped his ministrations. The intruder was Pappy Coyote. He needed their help with some minor crisis at the ranch. It was some years later before Clyde performed the ceremony again. His second attempt was infinitely more successful. This was the occasion when Clyde had allowed Shaman and Rachel to observe.

It had not been easy to find people who wanted to take part in the Ya Ya. Many feared the ancient rite, and many more had grown away from the old ways altogether. Clyde was even a little frightened by the tales he had heard of the power of this knowledge that few were privileged to have. Only Pappy Coyote and a handful of others joined him in the dance on this second occasion.

Clyde followed the ritual to the letter. He performed the dance and the animal chant and—donning his antelope skin—he pranced with the grace of a gazelle, leaping high above the flames of the bonfire. He felt an animal strength, smelled airborne scents from great distances and knew the ways of the animal world. The darkness cloaked his vision no more than a dusky veil. He walked on a bed of hot coals and felt no pain.

After that night, Clyde knew why his father had been so insistent in obtaining this power for his son. Many of Clyde's clients reaped the benefits of his newly found prowess. Opposition in the courtroom fell to the wayside like sheep before the mountain lion.

Those were heady times, even before he switched his specialty to criminal law. Now organized crime controlled even more wealth than international corporations, and they were willing to part with a substantial amount of it to remain on this side of a jail cell. Clyde was only too happy to oblige.

Clyde bounced the plane across the rough airfield, barely managing to brake the small jet in time to avoid the encroaching rocks. Yes," he murmured aloud, "it's time for a visit home."

He saw the lights of the antique farm truck approaching, and knew that Rachel would not be driving. He got out and ran to intercept his distant cousin, Pappy Coyote, his heart pounding in anticipation of bad news. Pappy handed him the note from Rachel.

Whatever the trouble was, it was evidently taking place at Keet Seel. Clyde grabbed a bag and his pilot's satchel from the plane. Shoving Pappy into the passenger seat, Clyde got behind the wheel of the vintage truck and pushed it to its limit. They stopped at the ranch only long enough for Clyde to don his desert clothes and plot a course to an abandoned airstrip near Tsegi Canyon. He called a Navaho friend who agreed to provide him with a horse at the designated landing site. Clyde and Pappy then sped back to the plane. Pappy once more ensconced behind the steering wheel of his beloved truck, covered his ears as the plane took to the skies once more.

CHAPTER XXI

Revelation

While Clyde raced toward Keet Seel, Zoe again slipped into an exhausted sleep. Beginning with their unexpected descent through the sipapu hole, Shaman related to Rachel all that had happened to him on his extraordinary journey. Rachel listened quietly. She was astounded at how many times she had made contact with him during his trials.

"Shaman, I've been monitoring your every ordeal. I saw the red-bellied snake. I even smelled the scent of Mariposa lilies. My mouth was parched when I awoke from meditating. I felt like I'd never get enough to drink. And of course, there's the water jar." She reached into her pack to produce an identical replica of Shaman's shattered savior. Shaman couldn't believe his eyes. Every detail was as he remembered.

Rachel's comforting presence had not been wishful thinking on his part. She had cradled his head after his close call with the huge reptile, and he had seen her as she molded the new jar while she meditated. Once more, Shaman's brain quickly rifled the files on restoring the vessel. He recalled that the ritual for replacing a magic water jar required the new container to be fashioned by a female relative. At least that part had been resolved. As the rest of the formula flashed across his memory, he wondered where he would find a large body of water in this desert.

"Rachel, I've learned what I am needed for. Now that the water jar has been returned, it is my task to restore its power. This source of pure water can be a beginning to healing the damage we've inflicted on the earth.

"I must also unmask the witch who is destroying the world's harmony. This two-heart is misusing the Ya Ya ceremony to assuage a personal greed. This avarice, cloaked in the power of the ritual, has been unleashed to enter the hearts and minds of men throughout the universe."

Rachel did not doubt him. She had seen the awesome power derived from the Ya Ya, and it frightened her. She was not surprised that people who could normally control their base emotions would have little defense against such power. No wonder the Earth was strangling in man's own greed.

"Shaman, Clyde is on his way. If anyone can help us find this witch, he can. He always has his ear to the ground, and many of the tribes owe him some debt of gratitude." No sooner had she spoken of their old friend than they heard him calling from outside their sanctuary. Shaman put Zoe in Rachel's arms and rushed to greet his blood-brother.

For the first time since he had seen that gaping black mouth swallowing his granddaughter, Shaman felt some degree of control. Not only had Rachel produced the required replica of the magic water jar, but she had brought Clyde as well. Somehow, between them, they would unravel this puzzle and put things right.

Zoe slept while the other three talked well into the night. They agreed that Shaman should stay at Keet Seel for the four day period of purification before attempting to restore the power of the water jar. Deciphering Clawing Bear's cryptic message about Kawestima could wait until after Shaman completed his first task.

Rachel and Zoe would return with Clyde to the ranch, and Clyde would continue on to New Mexico to do some sleuthing among his various acquaintances. Rachel planned to do the same locally, and she and Clyde would return in four days to decide the next plan of action. Clyde went to fetch his horse for the journey back to his plane. Rachel woke Zoe to say goodbye to her grandfather.

Zoe related her own adventures to her grandparents. They both shuddered when she told them of her plunge into the lake with the monster snake. Shaman remembered his own unnerving experience and was amazed at his granddaughter's courage. Rachel gave thanks that Zoe had not been taken from them.

As Zoe spoke of her final farewell to Alo, Rachel remembered the lady with the flashlight, and Shaman thought of the parting words from the receding fog, *"Hold my hand, and we'll walk together."*

Clyde returned with the horse. He put Rachel and Zoe astride, and they began the long walk back to the airstrip where, with the help of large battery lights, Clyde had landed his plane in the dark. His old friend was patiently waiting for Clyde's return. Clyde called the ranch to have someone meet them at the airstrip, helped his friend dismantle the lights, then they were heading home.

Shaman turned to the task ahead. The four days of purification would be the easy part. To replenish the power of the magic water jar, he must find a source of the original waters that once covered the Earth. The ritual also required an eagle feather, an eagle's wingtip, and sacred cornmeal. These three things had been provided during his journey to this place, but where could he find the body of water?

Shaman was in a deep state of meditation when he pictured himself floating down the disappearing Hassayampa River. Soon, he was not so much floating upon the waters but was an integral part of the river itself, flowing over and under the ground. He meandered with the river through the caverns beneath the kiva. Surely, somewhere beneath these ruins, he would find access to the great inland sea that lies beneath Arizona.

CHAPTER XXII

Rachel stared from the bedroom window into the gloomy morning light. She shook her head in disbelief, rubbed her eyes, and wondered how she could be standing here contemplating the existence of witches. Yesterday she would have approached the idea with mild amusement. Today she was deadly serious.

Until today, she had taken scant notice of a belief that many troubles are caused by two-hearts. A few hours ago she lumped witches with fortune-tellers and charlatans. Now she was convinced that the modern-day two-hearts were in control, and the world was in desperate trouble. Its salvation rested on the shoulders of a chosen few. She was one of the chosen, but at the moment, she was too exhausted to think straight. She turned from the window and headed for the old four-poster to grab a few hours of fitful sleep.

The morning light was easily held at bay by the overhang of the wrap-around porch. The Thomas ranch house had been built more than a century ago to withstand the heat of the sun's rays in an Arizona of the 1900s. In the twentieth century, its thick adobe walls, Saltillo tile floors, and narrow windows provided cool, dark shelter from the blazing sun. This morning Rachel left the draperies open, for today's sparse illumination would do little to hinder her nap.

It was nearly 2:00 p.m. when she finally roused. For the first time, Rachel felt her age. Glancing in the mirror of the huge armoire that occupied most of the wall space facing her bed, she noticed a few more gray hairs in the long, dark tresses. The face peering back at her was just beginning to register some small evidence of her advancing years.

I really should move that armoire. No woman should be subjected to a mirror the minute she wakes up, she thought.

Although she seldom dwelled on the encroaching evidence that she had passed middle-age, today she felt unusually vulnerable. Even the small wrinkles and tiny crow's feet made her doubt her ability to cope with her present task.

"Mirror, Mirror on the wall, who's the fairest Witch-hunter of them all?" she addressed her reflection in the mirror.

"I guess there really is no end to a woman's vanity." She scolded herself for being bothered by a gray hair or two when she had so much to do. "Rachel, old girl, you had better forget about how you look and concentrate on moving."

After prodding herself into action, Rachel showered and dressed in a soft, blue cotton skirt and matching blouse before slipping into her most comfortable sandals. She took one last, reassuring look at the attractive reflection in her armoire and felt her old self-confidence returning. She was now ready to find out all she could about the practice of witchcraft among the Indians.

She began sifting for details of half-remembered tales and legends of sorcery. Recalling Pappy's story about the two-heart, Rachel was not reassured. What she needed right now was a plan. How do you plan to catch a witch? Or is the proper term sorcerer?

"Maybe it's a whole coven," she thought aloud.

All her life, Rachel had heard the Indians muttering about the evil eye, but she never took their remarks any more seriously than an admonition not to walk under a ladder. She never threw spilled salt over her shoulder. She didn't believe that breaking a mirror will cause seven years bad luck. She would never dream of spitting on her crossed fingers to avoid the evil eye, nor did she believe that telling a bad dream will make it come true. These superstitions had probably been around since the beginning of time, but until today, she never thought much about them.

Surely, every society has its own irrational way of dealing with the unknown. When the rational laws of science fail to alleviate the anxieties of a group, that culture will invariably find relief in the supernatural, which often leads to a collective belief in charms and omens and magic potions.

From the recesses of her memory loomed Betatakin, stopping her theory in mid-thought. She wondered again why she and Shaman had not mentioned that kiva to anyone else. Without even discussing it, they each seemed to have decided that this place, with its almost palpable aura of evil, was best left alone. *Could we subconsciously believe that speaking our thoughts of a secret society with evil intent might give those thoughts substance?*

In all her years of studying ceremonial rites, Rachel had never been exposed to a ritual that was not done for the purpose of maintaining universal harmony.

She had seen rain clouds form in a previously cloudless sky, in answer to a village dance as old as memory. She had marveled when medicine men cured patients after conventional medicine did not work. This was not witchcraft; it was nature's answer to a spiritual outpouring of a deeply religious culture. She didn't totally understand the full import of mind over matter, but she believed in its existence. Indians routinely implemented its use to influence their world.

She decided to visit Harrison, the hand-trembler. This Navaho diagnostician still plied his trade in Canyon de Chelly, nurturing his herbs where the sun still broke through the pollution barrier on the exceptional day. Although he put great stock in his herbal concoctions, he believed that the ritual chant and sand paintings are as important as any medicinal applications.

He once told Rachel that his patients expected him to tell them what kind of illness they had, and whether it was from natural or supernatural causes; and since no medicine man could possibly know all the rituals—each being a specialist in one, or several, diseases—which singer could cure them.

If he can diagnose curses, then perhaps he knows who is responsible for them in the first place. Hadn't Pappy mentioned that he had heard the two-hearts might be meeting at Koyongtupqa(Canyon de Chelly)?

Rachel loaded the ever-faithful ranch truck with a few necessities. She left Zoe in the care of Pappy and his new wife, Hyacinth, and set out for the short journey. If Pappy was right, and something really was going on in the canyon, Harrison would know about it.

Chapter XXIII

Canyon De Chelly

By mid-afternoon Rachel was ensconced in her dusty room at the Thunderbird Lodge, an old tourist attraction that had become a landmark. Little had changed since her last visit. The bedspread was new. That was probably the extent of this year's efforts to refurbish. She was relieved to find that the plumbing was working. As much as she loved camping out, there were times when hot, running water and a toilet that flushes were dear to her heart. This was one of those times.

After showering and changing into fresh clothes, she went in search of Mike. The canyon guide was as much a fixture at the Thunderbird Lodge as Pappy Coyote was on their own ranch. Mike looked as old as some of the surrounding canyons, and he knew every inch of them. Every wash, cave, cliff, and surviving bush or animal were personally known to the antiquated pathfinder. He was the only one with whom Rachel would even consider traveling the canyon terrain at night.

The lodge had fallen into disrepair and the large, old cottonwoods that once graced its pathways were gone. As Rachel came down the walkway, she missed seeing their snowy seed-blossoms lying about the lawn.

Mike was just coming around one of the dilapidated corrals. She ran across the empty expanse of rocky earth that separated them, and didn't resist the urge to plant a kiss on that leathery old face.

She had never seen Mike in anything but denim jeans held up by a leather belt that sported the largest turquoise buckle she'd ever run across. God only knew how his skinny hips managed to keep gravity from pulling the weight of that buckle, jeans and all, down to the ankles of his snake-skin cowboy boots.

The toes of those boots were so pointed you could use them to excavate a mine. Mike's woolen shirt was long-sleeved, regardless of the weather, and buttoned to the kerchief-tied neck. His long, gray hair was tied beneath the feather-banded hat that shaded his chocolate eyes, indoors or out.

"Hello, Mike. You still look tougher'n whang and never a new wrinkle to show for the passing years," she said. He gave her one of his customary bear hugs.

"How could you find a new wrinkle among all these arroyos, anyhow? You're still a sassy gal, I reckon. Talk about wrinkles. How's come you never get any at all? Gal, don't you know how old you are? It ain't fittin' to look so young at your age. What brings you on a visit to these parts?"

Mike always sounded like a character in an old western, and after a visit with him, Rachel would usually pick up at least one new expression that was uniquely Mike's.

"Don't laugh, Mike, I'm witch-hunting."

"Say what, Gal?"

"I said, I'm witch-hunting, and I need your help. Have you heard of any strange rituals taking place out at Canyon de Chelly, or maybe up in Canyon del Muerto, maybe in the Mummy Cave?"

"You mean like black magic and such?"

"Well, something like that. Have you ever heard of the Ya Ya ceremony?"

"Sure, but that ain't black magic."

"What do you know about it?" Rachel asked.

"Well now, it's a Hopi ceremony, not Navaho. As best as I can recall, the story goes that some of the performers got so wrapped up in their powers that they started misusin' 'em, like magic tricks.

"I recollect some tales about folks using their powers to see far distances and inside of things, where they shouldn't oughta be able to. Then there was one story 'bout these fellers sittin' and paintin' the air in front of 'em while folks laughed at 'em, 'til them fellers pointed to a far cliff that all of a sudden had a new coat of white wash.

Mike continued, "The way I heard it, the last time anybody performed the Ya Ya, some of the things the participants could do after the ritual scared the bejesus outa most reg'lar folks. People got to callin' this power the evil eye. That ceremony kind of fell by the wayside after that. From the lack of critters around these days, it's too bad. We could use a little of that bringin'-the-critters-home power."

"I saw me a badger the other day. First one I've seen in three years. Sure do miss all the critters. I've still got these three mangy old swaybacks though, if you want to take a ride while you're here."

"Maybe tomorrow, Mike. Right now I was hoping you'd run me over to Harrison's place."

"Sure thing, gal, hop in the land rover over there. I'll be right with you."

Five minutes later, Rachel and Mike were on their way to the medicine man's hogan. Rachel was surprised that Mike's vehicle was not Betsy, his old Korean War vintage truck that had been prevalent in the late nineties for hauling tourists up and down the canyons.

"What happened to Betsy?" Rachel asked, while enjoying the smoother ride provided by the land rover. "I thought you two were wed for life."

"I had to put the old girl out to pasture. At her age, I couldn't ask her to take on the canyon anymore, but she's still up to a short haul now and then. It was her or me." Mike said, regretfully, and massaged his back. "My aging back requires a little more than old Betsy could supply in the shocks department. Don't have to worry so much about them blasted rocks anymore, neither. This baby has a much higher ground-clearance, too."

"I see it also has air filtering and water purification systems," Rachel remarked on some of the other accessories.

"These days, if you think you need it, you better take it with you. It's got back-up fuel, spare tires, and an extra air filter, too," Mike pointed out—proud as a new father.

As they disappeared in a trail of dust, a lone figure separated itself from the shadow of the lodge overhang and watched them depart.

Sadly, the new land rover wasn't the only change Rachel noticed. The stands of cottonwood, tamarisk, and Russian olives that once sheltered the Navaho farmers from the curious eyes of the tourists no longer existed. There was some shrubbery, but the little stone houses and mud hogans stood out starkly now against the backdrop of the great canyon walls.

Rachel found a little comfort in knowing that the ancient pueblo ruins tucked into the caves and overhangs of these canyons were still intact and would probably, like the sandstone cliffs, outlive man's foolishness.

They passed nature's own pictograph of a walking man superimposed from oxide stains high on the canyon wall. Most of the stains looked like old watermarks from past rains and runoffs, but this one was special. Just a short distance into the canyon, nature had drawn an Indian, as proud and straight as an ancient Egyptian, strolling by with his medicine bag strapped to his waist.

Mike veered toward the opposite wall to avoid a large stone, and Rachel admired the manmade pictographs that also commemorated man's passage through this great canyon.

They traveled deeper into the canyon before it split, Canyon de Chelly to the right, Canyon del Muerto to the left. They followed the wash to the left, heading for Black Rock Canyon beyond Navaho Fortress Rock. From force of habit, Mike repeated the information that he usually shared with tourists.

"You know, here in the 1800s, a small band of Navaho managed to climb this monolith, tryin' to evade capture by Kit Carson and his soldiers. Somehow they were able to struggle hundreds of feet up this sheer escarpment with enough sheep, vegetables, and water to sustain 'em for a period of weeks. To their surprise, the troops camped at the base of the rock didn't give up like the Navaho expected. Instead, the soldiers kept reinforcin' their numbers. They waited four months for the poor bastards to surrender. Those that didn't died of their wounds or starved to death. It was a sad state of affairs."

"It is a sad story," Rachel agreed. "But this relatively recent history is like yesterday compared to the stories depicted by the Anasazi. They left a timeless diary embedded in the pages of these canyon walls.

"Kit Carson was a modern-day Conquistador, riding through the canyon, bringing death and mayhem to the peaceful Pueblo farming communities," Rachel added.

Night was falling fast, and their interest in the canyon's history soon gave way to concentrating on their present ride. The road demanded Mike's full attention. Over the ages, streams had left deep depressions and areas of quicksand throughout the canyon floor. Mike wasn't one to take the canyon for granted. He respected its dangers.

While Mike concentrated on the driving, Rachel fought off a feeling of dread. The canyon seemed full of ghosts tonight.

When they finally arrived at the hand-trembler's hogan, they found a large crowd gathered. Mike went to inquire, returning to say they would have to wait for a while because an Enemy Way ceremony was being performed for a patient.

They made themselves comfortable in the land rover. Rachel passed the time by recalling what she knew of the Navaho Entah, or Enemy Way ritual. Once a purification ceremony for warriors, the Entah is performed for patients whose illness results from contact with non-Navahos, and it takes three days to complete the full ceremony.

A complicated ritual, intended to restore the patient to universal harmony and help him overcome the evils causing his maladies, it culminates with a mud bath, very similar to part of the ceremony that Shaman and Zoe witnessed at Old Oraibi. It's followed by a dance that lasts throughout the night.

Rachel could see that many people had gathered to participate in the ceremony. The food for those attending, plus the curing procedure itself, would be very costly to the patient and his family. Mike waited in silence for a few minutes before asking,

"You wanna tell me a little more about all this witch business?"

"It's kind of complicated," Rachel answered. "Shaman has had an extraordinary experience that has convinced him someone is using the Ya Ya ceremony for the purposes of witchcraft. This unleashing of greed has caused a universal disintegration of cosmic harmony. The witch must be unmasked, and the Ya Ya returned to its original intent. Then, maybe we can get a grip on repairing the damage already caused by our thoughtless self-gratification. Am I making any sense?"

"Sounds to me like you're sayin' we've messed the bed we sleep in, for nothin' more than a lack of good manners and a few bucks in our pockets. And it's all because we've been exposed to some powerful magic spell that's wrapped us in a blanket of greed. Is it possible that one feller's meanness could infect us all?"

"Why not, we can spread hatred and distrust as easily as a contagious disease. Or we can use a little good will to surround ourselves with smiles. With humanity's predilection for greed, I can believe that a whole world culture could be contaminated, when the ill wind that spreads it is as powerful as the Ya Ya and as old as time. The person using the ritual may not even be aware of its long-range potential."

There was a light tap on the driver's window. Harrison was standing in full regalia beside their vehicle. A true aficionado of ancient ways, Harrison shunned modern dress during ceremonies, opting for a more traditional costume of skins, feathers, rattles, and a terrifying head-dress.

"Sorry, friends, but this is going to take a while. I won't be finished here until tomorrow night. Is there something I can do for you, quickly?"

"Can you meet me at the Thunderbird Lodge the day after tomorrow? I've got something important to talk to you about. I don't think I can cover it in a couple of minutes," Rachel answered.

"That's a sure thing. Look for me around seven a.m. OK?"

"That's great. Just one thing before we leave. Are there any ceremonies being held in the canyon that you know of?"

"Nothing for sure, but you might take a look around Martini Cave. I've heard some chants and the like coming from that area a few times."

"Thanks, I'll see you the day after tomorrow. Hope you have a successful curing."

As Harrison retreated into the darkness, Rachel turned to Mike. "I assume you can find your way to Martini Cave in the dark. If you don't mind, I'd like to take a look tonight."

"Sure, it's one of my favorite places. It's still dry as a bone with a hell of a hangover, or is that overhang?" It was an old joke, but Mike never missed a chance to repeat it. A hundred yards from the cave, they could hear a light cadence. They moved closer. The cadence became a low, rhythmic drumbeat, and a staccato "Yah hi hi," followed by "Huh, Huh." Mike was not familiar with the sounds, but Rachel was. The hairs on the nape of her neck were standing on end as she relived the hypnotic chant of the Ya Ya.

"I don't think we'd better drive any closer, Mike. Let's get out and see if we can get a little nearer on foot." Mike disabled the interior light before opening his door. Night, almost palpable, crept in the driver's door while Rachel prepared to exit from the other side. Before she could pop the door handle, she heard Mike grunt. She turned and saw his body slump forward against the wheel. As she bent over to grab his arm, an arrow whizzed through the interior of the land rover and lodged itself where her head had been resting a split second ago.

Without stopping to think, Rachel jammed her foot on the accelerator and shifted into drive, causing the land rover to lurch forward. The driver's door swung shut, and Mike's body flopped like a car-crash mannequin. She managed to get her hands on the steering wheel and turned it hard left. Mike's body shifted enough to give her control.

They barely escaped running headlong into the canyon wall before Rachel succeeded in getting them turned and headed back the way they had come. No more missiles came hurtling at them from the dark, so she braked long enough to make sure the doors were locked, and felt for a pulse at Mike's flaccid wrist.

He was unconscious, but he was alive. Sitting almost atop of the dying man, and disregarding pot holes and hazards, Rachel raced back toward the Thunderbird Lodge. Hell-bent on saving Mike's life, she didn't even notice her own blood pouring from a gash caused by her head hitting the roof. When she finally stopped, car horn blaring, at the lodge's front door, she was holding the steering wheel so tightly she couldn't let go.

The front desk clerk heard the commotion and rushed to the driver's door and tried to open it. Rachel finally wrenched one hand free to unlock the door. The young Navaho attendant was astonished by the sight of Rachel—still gripping the steering wheel with one hand—sitting in Mike's lap, in a pool of blood.

Rachel screamed, "It's an emergency! Get an ambulance and some help out here!" Her own high-pitched hysteria stirred her to action, and she managed to get out of the vehicle and inspect Mike's wound. There was an arrow jutting from the left side of his neck. It had entered at an angle, continuing its downward path to rest under the left clavicle. Rachel applied pressure and prayed that the jugular vein had not been pierced. There was an enormous amount of congealing blood, his and hers. While maneuvering out of the canyon, she had inadvertently managed to smear them both from head to foot. Mike was alive, but just barely.

CHAPTER XXIV

Keet Seel

Shaman and Zoe had ended up at Keet Seel by way of the keyhole-shaped kiva located on one of the three streets that serviced the nearly eight-hundred-year-old village. The hole through which he and Zoe had emerged was once again no more than a symbolic reproduction of the original sipapu hole.

Sham had more than a passing acquaintance with this kiva. It had been remarkably well preserved, boasting a sandstone slab floor and plastered walls painted with wide, white bands. There was a large rectangular pit near the usual fireplace. While archaeologists had never been able to agree on the purpose of this pit, all did agree that Keet Seel seemed to have been inhabited by a more diversified population than the typical ruin.

Shaman knew there were at least four kivas in the village, all distinctively different, and at least one building was a two-story tower in the Mesa Verde style. Many other rooms had been built and abandoned, only to have their beams salvaged to be used again in newer accommodations portraying a different architectural concept.

The Anasazi of Keet Seel had built a retaining wall at the mouth of the cave. Here, they dumped their refuse. Upon this landfill, they eventually added more buildings. At the village's peak, the cave overhang sheltered over one hundred and fifty rooms, probably housing about that same number of people.

Surprisingly, only nine burial sites had ever been located to account for the dead of Keet Seel. What happened to the remainder of the occupants? Sealed granaries full of corn were left behind by some of the inhabitants. It would seem that, as similarly evidenced at other ruins, the people expected to be returning to their stores. The water table here had dropped dramatically over the last century, leaving little more than stunted sagebrush and snake weed as surviving vegetation.

Sham chose to begin the purification rites in the keyhole kiva. His last thoughts before losing himself in meditation were concerned with his instructions to restore the magic water jar. According to legend, the jar must be carried to a large body of water that has covered the Earth since the beginning of the Fourth World. There, the jar carrier must use an eagle feather and sacred cornmeal to complete the necessary prayers. He must use an eagle's wingtip to collect certain ingredients from the sand and water and place them in the newly replicated jar. These things are required to enable the container, when planted in the earth, to bring water to any area, no matter how arid the land might be.

The fact remained that Sham must first locate something resembling an ocean. As his mind drifted deeper into meditation, the sounds of a rushing river filled his ears. The spirit fog returned, its long tendrils snaking up through the sipapu hole in the center of the kiva. Shaman's mind soared free as his body was engulfed by the soft moisture.

CHAPTER XXV

Visions

Rachel sat at the bedside in the little clinic room, close enough to touch Mike's clammy skin repeatedly and be reassured by the thready pulse heralding the blood transfusions coursing through his veins. She finally drifted into an exhausted sleep, and did not notice the stealthy fog creeping slowly above her ankles, enfolding the hospital bed and its sleeping attendant within its misty cocoon.

Waking at about 3:00 a.m., Rachel turned to inspect her patient. She took faint notice of the receding mist that was dissipating on the clinic floor. Mike's eyes opened briefly. He made an effort to produce a smile of reassurance. Though more of a grimace than a smile, Rachel was ecstatically happy to see it. Even though the doctor had told her hours ago that Mike would recover, she couldn't leave his side until he regained consciousness.

The attack had come as a total surprise. Who could possibly know they were in the canyon? There must have been sentries posted to protect the participants of the ritual being performed beneath the immense protective overhang at the base of the canyon wall. She had told no one but Pappy her destination. In spite of the hour, she phoned the ranch to check on Zoe.

"Yes ma'am, Zoe is sleeping right next to me," said Hyacinth. "She didn't want to be alone, so I'm sleeping in the big bed with her."

"Did anyone come by or call?"

"Just mister Clyde called to make sure everything was all right, and he said to tell you he might have a lead. He'll be checking it out tomorrow, and he'll get back to you as soon as he's sure. Do you want me to tell him anything special when he calls?"

"Yes, tell him to call me at the Thunderbird. If I'm not in, he should leave the number where he can be reached. I'll call him as soon as I can. Take care of Zoe. I should be home in a couple of days."

Mike returned to a recuperative sleep, and Rachel left to make her way back to the lodge. The double bed seemed especially empty without Shaman, and she mentally reached out in the hope of locating him somewhere in that realm of semi-conscious slumber. In a moment, she heard the sound of running water, and felt herself slipping into the liquid world of a vast sea. She was oblivious to a furtive fog rising to engulf the bed.

In her slumber, Rachel drifted like a tadpole floating in the undercurrents of the great sea. A sudden upheaval of the ocean floor left her swimming below a rising land mass as it pushed far above the receding ocean. Soon she drifted aimlessly through the cooler pools beneath the newly formed mountains and valleys above, winding her way from cavern to cavern as the waters flowed inexorably on a downward path. The sea settled its greatly reduced volume in a new subterranean home. Here Rachel experienced the passing of uninterrupted eons of time.

In her subterranean eddy, the carving of the great canyons went as unnoticed to Rachel as the developing plant and animal life. While the world above her protective sea molded itself from the elements of creation, the passing fancies of sun and wind left no mark here within the remaining volume of the mother waters.

As Rachel communed with creation, the hours passed, broken only by the appearance of a dark shadow outside her window. There was a light tap at her door, loud enough to rouse her from her slumber. A key turned in the lock, and Rachel called from her bed, "Who's there?"

"It's the maid. Excuse me, but do you want your room cleaned today?" Rachel noticed the time was late afternoon as she invited the young Navaho maid to come in.

"You can leave fresh towels. That's all I need for now."

"I'm sorry I woke you. When I saw the man walking away, I didn't think anyone was in here," the maid said.

"What man was that?" asked Rachel.

"I just finished the room next door. As I was bringing out the dirty linens, I saw a man hurry away. I thought he came from this room. I must have been mistaken. Maybe he knocked on your door, and you just didn't hear."

Rachel didn't think so. After all, she had heard the maid's light tap, hadn't she?

"What did he look like," Rachel asked. "Was he a local?"

"I didn't know him, so I don't think he's from around here. I'm not even sure he was Navaho. He could have been, but I didn't get a very good look at him. Were you expecting someone?"

"Not until tomorrow. If it was Harrison, I think you would have recognized him."

"You mean the hatathli. Yes, I would know the singer. He was not the man at the door. Are you sure you don't want me to clean the room?"

"Yes, I'm sure. I've hardly been in it enough to make any mess, but if you have a few moments to spare, I'd like to talk to you."

"No problem. If it's a choice between cleaning and talking, I can rattle on all day. Are you interested in something special? I live in Chinle, (Chin-lee) so I know the answers to most tourist questions."

"Maybe we should start with introductions. My name is Rachel."

"I'm Mary."

"Please, have a seat, Mary. What I want to talk about isn't exactly a tourist question, but it does relate to Native American folklore and customs. I've been a student of Indian culture all my life, and I know that many of the tribes believe in witches. Do you? Can you tell me anything about them?"

"Well, I'm Catholic myself," said Mary, "but I think a lot of Christians believe in witches, too. Some people seem to be born with powers that most of the rest of us don't have. These aren't people you want to get on the bad side of."

"Would a witch be able to use the power of a religious ceremony like the Hopi Ya Ya for their own purposes?" Rachel asked.

"From what I know of the Hopi ceremonies, it wouldn't be easy to learn the secrets of any of them. It's not like they have a catechism to study, and the Ya Ya would be especially secretive because of the magical powers it can produce. It's supposed to give the dancers great strength and the ability to see and hear like animals. Some people believe it actually turns the dancers into the animals they imitate. It wouldn't be easy to subvert a ritual as powerful as the Ya Ya."

"Then you think it would have to be a Hopi to get access to the ritual?"

"Probably," Mary answered thoughtfully. "The Hopi don't even share the secrets of their ceremonies with other Hopi clans. Although a witch can do things most people can't. I don't actually know any witches," she hastened to add, "but Catholic or not, I always carry the medicine bag my grandmother made for me. I figure it can't hurt," she added with a little smile.

"I guess we need all the help we can get," Rachel said sincerely. "Well, thanks for the chat. I won't keep you from your work any longer."

The young maid left, and Rachel decided to try the gift shop for any written material that might be available on the subject. She remembered the mysterious visitor and took a quick look in both directions before leaving her room. No one was about. She could hear Mary humming as she made up the room next door. I wouldn't mind having my own medicine bag about now, she thought.

The bookstore had a lot of tourist information, but nothing much on the rites of witchcraft. Rachel wasn't surprised. Witchcraft was hardly a subject that curious tourists would find relaxing.

The best she could find was a book called The Hopi Way, a collection of stories that included a number of tales concerning witches or sorcerers. Some of the other ceremonial literature did make brief references to ill winds and the evil eye, but gave no specific details.

Responding to the hunger pangs which had been trying to get her attention for some time, Rachel hurried the few steps to the cafeteria and ordered vegetable stew and fry bread. She loved the pizza-sized bread with its calorie soaked exterior, and since the inside consisted mostly of air pockets, she rationalized the extent of the damage it might cause her arteries. The stew was under-seasoned, as usual, but that was easily remedied by the salt and pepper shakers.

As she ate, she wondered how Shaman was doing. She worried that he was getting a little over the hill for a four day fast. It had been almost two days already, and all she had managed to accomplish was to get an old friend nearly killed and confirm the fact that some Indians do indeed believe in the power of witchcraft. Today, so did she.

CHAPTER XXVI

Underground Sea

———◆———

Shaman had not moved from the sipapu hole in the keyhole kiva. In a near trance, he saw a receding tendril of fog beckoning him to the Netherworld. The sipapu hole, like a sleeping giant's yawn, was slowly enlarging. Sham collected the items that he would need for the restoration ritual and gently lowered himself into the hole and descended the wooden ladder to the bottom of the cavern below.

Very little light penetrated from the opening above. Shaman judged that he had previously entered this place from the left of where he was now standing, but when he looked into the shadows, there was only a blank sandstone wall. He closed his eyes and concentrated on using only his inner eye. In a moment he could see clearly, and moved directly to the hidden opening from which Zoe had emerged to be reunited with him.

Shaman opened his eyes, then closed them once more. *When my eyes are open, I'm so aware of the blackness it's like a physical restraint, limiting my ability to move. When I close them, the blackness becomes only space, and I can see everything clearly.*

Sham traversed several adjoining caverns before he heard rushing water. In the next room, he came upon the source of the sound, and followed the flow of the river toward its ultimate destination.

There was a large boulder on his left. Cave crickets echoed their shrill chirps off the cavern walls. Something beneath the rock caught his attention. Sham approached the huge mass of stone. He recognized the remains of a human form. One leg of the skeleton was pinned beneath the rock's massive weight.

The departed Anasazi's skull was intact. It even had one long lock of dark hair still attached. The feet were encased in sandals woven of yucca fiber, squared at the toes and tied at the ankles. Still draped around the bony waist was a medicine bag made of rolled cornhusks. It was held together with a cord of yucca fiber and attached to the remnants of a hide loincloth. As Shaman contemplated this find, an apparition manifested itself by the ancient skeleton.

"Greetings, Shaman," said the ghostly image. There was little left that could surprise Sham now, so he simply replied.

"Hello, have we met?"

"Yes, we have. Though you might remember me better if I were brandishing a spear," answered the friendly specter.

"Ah yes, it was you who abandoned me to the mercies of the sea of reptiles. How could I ever forget?"

"I hope you harbor no ill feelings. We each have our own duties to perform, do we not?"

"You know, you sound a lot less Indian now than you did then," Sham responded.

"I do not know of Indian or other. Do you think you sound different because you are only part-Indian? What does a part-White man sound like? Do they all sound the same as you? I shall be happy to appear as you wish. Is there some particular persona that you would prefer?"

"No, be what you wish. I understand your words. That's sufficient. This is all a new experience to me. Is there anything special that I should do?" asked Sham.

"Do you know why you are here?"

"I think I am expected to restore a magic water jar, and then I must attempt to unmask a witch. Does that sound reasonable to you?"

"You've put it rather succinctly. I doubt I could have done better myself. Your first task is to finish the job that I failed to complete several hundred years ago. I would also like to congratulate you on the way you handled that first little test."

This is definitely a very friendly ghost, thought Sham. "I appreciate the flattery, but what I'd really like is a little navigational help. Where were you off to when you were so rudely interrupted by that boulder?"

"Nicely put, my friend. I was following the river from the great sea. As caretaker of the magic water jar, I had been remiss in my duties. It wasn't like I conjured up that earthquake, but had I been more attentive, I might have been able to salvage the jar before it was shaken to bits.

"I knew all the right things to do to restore it, of course. My mother fashioned another jar. I was returning from your present destination, and except for this unfortunate occurrence, the Hisatsinom; or maybe you know them as Anasazi, might have been able to withstand the long drought."

Sham felt a slight tug of guilt at this last remark, for he often used the word Anasazi, even though he knew it was a Navaho term.

"I'm sorry, I'm sure most of us don't mean to be offensive," he said. "But the name the Navaho have given the Old Ones is the one popularly used today. Very little is written about the Hisatsinom, but there is a glut of information available on the Anasazi."

"I know," the spirit remarked. "Some of it is even accurate. I'm glad the world hasn't forgotten us. I just don't relish being called an ancient enemy. But that's history. You're doing the best you can with what you have to work with. After all, we've been gone a long time, and our few descendants are rather reclusive.

"I did have one visitor, though. By the way you reckon time, it would have been about two hundred years ago. The scoundrel stole my water jar. He was in and out before I knew it. But I guess I'm being too hard on the fellow. He probably thought it was just another pot. At least he was Indian, as you might say. As a matter of fact, the jar you're carrying is a replica of it. I conjured the original of that one up for your first test of knowledge. I'm surprised you didn't recognize it."

"Why? Should I have?" asked Shaman.

"Well, maybe not. Most young people don't pay a lot of attention to their physical surroundings, but I'm sure you must have been exposed to it somewhere along the way," answered the spirit.

"Enough about me, the spirit continued. Now, let's see about that navigational help. Leave no prints, do no damage and let the river guide you. Nice talking to you, Sham." At that, the apparition vanished, leaving only a skeleton, half hidden beneath a boulder.

Not exactly a road map, thought Sham, but he trudged on, an eagle feather in his left hand, an eagle's wingtip in his right, and Rachel's newly formed jar under his arm. After entering and exiting several more caverns, Sham came upon a special cave, the floor of which was virgin flowstone. He remembered the admonition of the ill-fated water-jar carrier.

"Leave no prints."

Sham knew he could not walk upon this malleable stone without leaving the imprint of his steps, yet there was no path or ledge to circumnavigate the impressionable floor. The river became the only choice to continue on his present route. As he prepared to tread the water, he remembered more of the apparition's warning.

Do no damage. Could he possibly damage anything by swimming to the next cavern?

"Better safe than sorry," he muttered to himself while stripping off his garments to avoid leaving any small residue of contamination. He entered the river, taking care to hang on tightly to the three prized objects, and paddled toward the hole in the cavern wall through which the river flowed.

The adjoining cave took his breath away. Cautious not to touch a single configuration, he moved between mammoth gypsum deposits as white and delicate as snowflakes. Large veins of crystal in patterns more intricate than spider webs decorated the walls. Maneuvering between those flows that could be imprinted by his passing, he once again walked upon solid ground. He found the walls of the next room even more stunning. Shaman's senses were overwhelmed by the wonderful renditions of animals of bygone centuries.

"Do you like those?" asked the now-familiar apparition who had materialized again by his side. Sham studied a mammoth charging a great ochre beast with a hairy mane and a long-toothed tiger stalking its prey across the walls of the cave.

"Lovely," said Shaman. "I didn't hear you enter. Is this your work?"

"I'm not much for flashy entrances," Sham's new acquaintance explained. "In reply to your question, don't I wish? Whoever drew them really knew his craft. I used to sit and study them until it would seem that they were running straight at me. I could almost feel their hot breath and hear their animal grunts."

The apparition imitated these sounds with a deep, breathy "Huh, Huh." Then he continued, "No, these are thousands of years older than I. Most of those behemoths were already extinct before my time. But I like to come just to admire them. This is the first time I've had a chance to share them with anyone. You know, this wasn't exactly a heavily traveled thoroughfare in my day."

"I can appreciate that," Sham sympathized. "I wonder if the artist had an audience with whom he could share this display. I'd like to think so. At any rate, I'm quite impressed."

"For the artist, I thank you for your kind words. If you wouldn't mind, I'd like to accompany you to your journey's end," implored Sham's new friend.

"The company would be much appreciated," said Shaman. The next cavern widened until they could not see the boundaries. They were standing by a great underground sea, with only horizon before them. The Hisatsinom sighed and turned to face Shaman directly.

"You don't know how pleased I am to have met you," he said, extending his hand palm up.

"And I, you," answered Shaman as he gripped the upturned palm in the age-old acknowledgment of friendship and understanding. With that, his companion vanished.

Shaman knelt in the ripples at the water's edge and recited the prayers that were required before he could plant his paho and collect the ingredients to restore the power of the magic water jar.

CHAPTER XXVII

Retrospect

Rachel found a police detective in Mike's room. It was Billy Dillon, a young Navaho whose family she had known for years.

"Mrs. Thomas, good to see you." Billy stood when she entered. "I tried to call you at the lodge, but you were out. Mike can't do much talking for a while, so I'd sure appreciate a statement from you. Last night, the doctor said you were in a state of shock yourself, and you were asleep when I looked in. I thought maybe we could both get some shut-eye before I bothered you. I figured you wouldn't be going anyplace 'til Mike is better." Billy offered his chair to Rachel and pulled up another for himself.

"I'm afraid I can't be of much help, but I'll tell you what I can. We were near Martini Cave when someone shot Mike through the throat with an arrow. I never saw who it was. I don't even remember thinking at all. It happened so fast. All I could do was get us out of the canyon. There was so much blood everywhere. I knew Mike needed medical attention immediately."

"What were you doing in the canyon after dark? That's pretty dangerous terrain at night."

"We went to Black Rock to visit with Harrison, the hand trembler. He was busy with a ceremony, so we left.

"Yeah, I got that much from the doc. I've already been out to Martini Cave. Why did you go there?" Billy probed.

"You know I have a great interest in Indian ceremonies, Billy. Someone mentioned that there might be a ritual taking place in that area. I just thought we'd take a look while we were in the neighborhood. When we heard what sounded like chanting, Mike opened the door to listen. The next thing we knew, arrows were whizzing at us, and Mike was hit. When you checked out the cave, were there any signs that a ceremony had been held recently?"

"Yeah, someone had been there. Whoever it was took off in a hurry. They left behind some pahos and a piece of a coyote hide that got caught on one of those big, dead branches from an old cottonwood.

"Sounds like somebody doesn't want company at their ceremony," he continued. "They've sure got a nasty way of getting the message across. It could be another of those black magic groups that never seem to go away. Some strange types find these canyons appealing. You'd be surprised how many lost souls are out there looking for a quick answer."

A nurse slipped in soundlessly and took Mike's vital signs. He never stirred. She gave Rachel and Billy a smile and assured them he was doing well, before slipping away as silently as she had come. Billy hesitated for a moment before broaching another subject.

"You know, Ma'am. I read the old report once on that incident when your husband's parents were killed. It's never made any sense to me. Your ranch is fairly isolated out there, but you'd think someone would eventually have learned something about that night. It sure wasn't a burglary. Nothing was reported missing. Every pot in the house was smashed to bits, but vandalism doesn't usually lead to murder." Rachel nodded in agreement. Billy continued his case-folder litany.

"At first everybody assumed Mr. and Mrs. Thomas had put up quite a struggle, until the coroner's report negated that theory. The bodies showed no signs of having resisted. There weren't any cuts on the victims. They were shot from close range and left for dead. That's always made me think that the killer was somebody they knew.

"I'd say they were probably shot before the killer went through the house, breaking all the pottery. That'd be really cold, destroying that collection while Mr. and Mrs. Thomas lay dying in the foyer. Did your husband ever have any ideas about all that?"

Billy reddened. He hadn't meant to imply that Shaman was in any way a suspect. Billy was a good policeman. He had the highest rank of anyone with only five years of experience on the force, but, in his enthusiasm for a case, things sometimes didn't come out just the way he meant to say them.

"I don't mean to infer that he'd have any answers, Ma'am. It's just academic. I worked for a little while with a detective by the name of Osinski. He used to talk about it all the time. Any loose ends on a case would drive him crazy. This was one that had him totally baffled until the day he passed away," Billy apologized.

"It's OK, Billy. I don't mind your asking." Rachel smiled to put her young inquisitor at ease. "No, Shaman never had any idea who could have done such a terrible thing. When the investigation was active, the police thought it was most likely a transient, maybe someone high on dope. Shaman had no reason to disagree."

"Yeah, he's probably right. That's one of the theories Detective Osinski came up with, too. Sure is strange, though." Billy steered the conversation back to the present mystery. "Nothing else you can add about last night's attack?" Rachel mulled it over before replying.

"Not really, but if I think of anything, I'll call." With that, Billy said goodbye, leaving Rachel to ponder his questions. The drawn drapes filtered any light that might stray into the sickroom where Mike lay. Rachel sat quietly in the darkened room. She listened to the steady rhythm of Mike's breathing and tried to recall everything Sham had ever told her about that fateful night in 2010. Tears filled Rachel's eyes as she thought of Shaman sitting by his mother's bedside and holding her hand as it grew colder.

CHAPTER XXVIII

Deathbed

Rachel would never forget Shaman's description of that night.

Nurse Warden responded immediately to the Code Three alert that the monitoring device had signaled to the nursing station, but there was nothing the resuscitation team could do to revive Deborah Thomas. The team withdrew from the intensive care unit. Shaman was left alone to say his good-byes to the woman who had loved and raised him.

Sham's heartbeat quickened when his mother's hand closed on his. He waited expectantly, but it had been only a reflexive action that often occurs as the body temperature cools after death.

Sometime later, the nurse returned and gently suggested that Shaman let them take care of the deceased. He knew there were things that needed to be done to lessen the effects from the onset of rigor mortis, so he reluctantly said his final good-bye to his mother and headed for the bowels of the hospital.

Sham concentrated on the elevator light while he played the familiar mind game that he had developed to associate people with their names. The nurse's tag had identified her as Ms. Warden. A synonym for warden could be escort. The name was aptly chosen. The small pink bundle delivered to the Wardens had been destined to spend her years escorting the dying across that last step into the unknown.

The interminably slow elevator finally chimed its arrival, and Sham brought his mind back to the gruesome errand that still awaited him in the morgue. He stepped inside and pressed the button for the basement. He had never visited a hospital morgue that wasn't hidden away in the bowels of the building.

Morgues always gave him goose bumps. He investigated human remains as a matter of course, but there was a comfortable degree of detachment in handling the skeleton recovered from a thousand year old grave. If only a moment ago he had felt the pulse or held the frightened hand of the corpse he was assessing, he would not be able to attain that detachment.

The elevator stopped, opened its automatic mouth, and Sham found himself spat out, staring at the door to the hospital's anatomy lab. He took a deep breath, straightened his shoulders and stepped through the door.

A white-jacketed lab technician greeted him before picking up the telephone to page Detective Osinski. Sham paced nervously in the reception room. The seating area was not what he would ordinarily picture for a morgue. It was carpeted in the same soft shade as the lavender walls that reflected a warm, soothing light. Upholstered armchairs were arranged about the room. Detective Osinski arrived a moment later.

"Are you OK?" He didn't like the kid's color. "We can do this a little latter if you want."

"Thanks, but I'll be fine." Sham followed as the detective shuffled down a narrow hall.

The rotund Osinski stopped at an elongated window-pane and pressed a button beneath it. An attendant appeared on the other side of the glass, waited for the Detective to flash his police credentials, then pulled the blinds to reveal a draped corpse lying on a gurney.

Osinski looked at Shaman. "Are you ready?"

Sham nodded, and Osinki motioned for the attendant to pull down the sheet to display the deceased for viewing.

Rigor mortis had started to take its toll. The features were stiff and drawn, but the red hair and high cheekbones were unmistakably those of his father. What he saw in the face of the cadaver was a distorted mirror-image of himself.

"Do you need more time, Shaman?" Osinski asked kindly.

"No. That's my father, William Thomas." The name came hard to his lips, but somehow it was easier to accept the still, gray corpse as the remains of a man named William Thomas than one called Dad.

Sham did not want to view his father's body more completely. He knew what a gun blast at close range could do to a human being. His father was gone. Shaman preferred to mourn him elsewhere.

He accompanied Detective Osinski back to the ranch to see if he could tell if anything was missing. From the time they entered the front door, pottery shards littered the whole of the house. Not one piece of his mother's marvelous pot collection was left intact. It was as if some maniac with an aversion to clay had shot Sham's parents and gone on a rampage. His mother's jewelry was intact. The silver was in its storage box, and as far as he could tell, nothing was missing.

"How did you find them?" Sham asked.

"One of the ranch-hands called it in. He was returning from a ceremony of some sort, saw the front door open. Since most everyone from the ranch had gone to the same doings, your parents were alone. Your mom and dad were found in the foyer.

"The guy thought they were both dead, but then your mom made a sound, and he called for an ambulance. The forensics team has already been here, but I don't hold out much hope that they'll turn up any clues. It's one of the strangest things I've ever seen.

"You know there'll have to be autopsies, but the pathologist said his preliminary examination indicated that there hadn't been any struggle."

"Did my mother say anything at all?"

"The ranch-hand said she asked for water, but as far as I know, that was the only word she spoke. Was she able to tell you anything?"

"No," said Sham. "She was only half-conscious. I think she was just waiting for me to get here so she could say good-bye." Sham had stayed at the ranch long enough to make the burial arrangements. He attended the inquest that established that his parents had been murdered by a person or persons unknown. The forensic pathologist confirmed his preliminary findings; death by gunshot, with no sign of resistance. Detective Osinski pursued the case for many years, but no other clues were ever found.

Sham had also confided to Rachel the strange experience he'd had in the library before making the call that had brought him the news that his parents had been shot. This was not, he explained, the first time he had been overcome by some strange feeling of precognition, but it was, by far, the one with the worst consequences.

For some time afterwards, Rachel avoided going into the basement archives, although Sham continued to work at his favorite old wooden desk.

CHAPTER XXIX

Revelation

Mike was clearly out of danger, sleeping peacefully and regaining some of his color.

Rachel returned to her hotel room. The brown chintz draperies looked more Aztec than Navaho, and they didn't quite match the new bedspread. She waited for Clyde's call. She was anxious to talk to Harrison in the morning. It was obvious that something was going on in the canyon, and Harrison was her best bet to discover who was involved. A few minutes later the phone rang.

"Hello, Rachel, have you had any luck?" Clyde asked.

"Yes, there's some bad news and some worse news. The bad news is, there is definitely some sort of ritual being held here. The worse news is that Mike Littlefoot, while trying to get me close enough to see what was going on, got an arrow through his neck. He's going to be all right. It was a close call. I'll tell you all about it when I see you. Can you add anything from your end?"

"Not much. I thought I had a lead, but it turned out to be just a crazy hermit who claims to be a prophet. I'm surprised at how many new-age ceremonials are out there. It seems that any good vision worth its salt today can be turned into a full-fledged ceremony."

Clyde continued, "Some of these new rituals can get pretty weird. They're all supposed to endow their practitioners with some exceptional power, but so far, they're all directed towards communal harmony. I guess I'm getting old. I prefer the old rituals that have been handed down for centuries. There are a few so-called witches in the weeds, but no one to take seriously; just a couple of magic-trick conjurers and love-potion hustlers out to impress their neighbors or make a couple of bucks off of some minor ritual."

"Well, thanks for the update," said Rachel. "I'm going to be seeing Harrison tomorrow morning. Hopefully, he'll be able to give me a line on this thing. I want to get home sometime tomorrow if I can. I need to check on Zoe before I head back up to Keet Seel."

"Don't worry about that. I'll be flying out tomorrow. I'll look in on her," offered Clyde. "I'm not getting anywhere here. Sounds like you're on to something there, so do whatever you need to, and I'll catch up with you. I have an early morning meeting with some high-powered Pillsbury types, but I'll head out right after that. You take care now. I'll see you sometime tomorrow."

After hanging up, Rachel prepared for sleep. As she was drifting off, she thought about how lucky they were to have a good friend like Clyde.

Not many people would be out witch-hunting at the drop of a fetish. It's too bad he doesn't have any close family now that both his parents are gone. Of course he's part of our family, but it would be nice if he had someone of his very own.

Rachel awakened later than usual for her. She jumped in and out of the shower, dressed and called room-service for a pot of coffee and toast for two. She briefly considered indulging in more fry bread, but her arteries cringed, and she decided to have mercy on them. Breakfast arrived at the same time as Harrison.

"Yat ta heh," said Harrison, using the customary Navaho greeting, while carrying in the room-service tray. "I heard what happened the other night. Sorry I sent you up there."

"Yat ta heh," she returned his greeting. "It wasn't your fault. There are some very unfriendly people in that canyon, and they're doing something they'd rather no one knew about. Do you have any idea what's involved?"

"I've been asking around, and I've heard some rumors about a new and powerful ritual being developed over the last few years. It's supposed to have started around the turn of the century. It's been recruiting new followers right along. It sounds a lot like the Hopi Ya Ya."

Harrison continued, "Everybody is pretty secretive about the whole thing, but the rumor mill asserts that all the participants end up pretty well-off. It's hard to believe, but supposedly, not one practitioner has died of natural causes in that length of time."

As Harrison informed her of this, he helped himself to coffee and a slice of toast. With an anticipatory gleam in his eye, he smothered the toast under an inch of peach preserves.

"I shall forever be grateful to the Hopi for bringing peaches to Canyon de Chelly," he mumbled as he inhaled the sweet sandwich.

"Do you have any idea at all who the head priest in this new religion is?" Rachel asked.

"Not a clue. But he must have had some pretty strong magic to convince others of the ritual's power. Most folks are pretty happy with the ceremonies that have been handed down from their ancestors. There's always a little skullduggery going on, of course, but between a curing way and the clinic, normally nothing we can't handle."

Rachel gave Harrison a brief explanation of what had been happening over the last few days. She concluded her story with the fact that Shaman, in preparation for the restoration of the water jar, was fasting at Keet Seel.

"I've heard the Hopi legend of the magic water jar," said Harrison, "but I always thought it was just a myth. If Sham really has his hands on a magic water jar, that'd be pretty powerful medicine to a lot of people. There's still a few of the older Hopi who talk about moving back to their homes in Keet Seel. Don't seem to make them no never-mind that that's Navaho country now."

"Harrison, I'm sure there's a connection somewhere between the water jar and the death of Sham's parents. I've been thinking about it a lot. The night they were killed, someone destroyed all the pots in the house. Did you ever see his mother's pottery collection?"

"Yeah, I was just a kid. Sham was away at college. I remember because I was wishing he was there to pitch a few balls to me. I wasn't really into pot collections, but I recall it was pretty magnificent. Some of those pieces were centuries old. The old lady had salvaged a lot of them from roadside hustlers, but most had been handed down from her own grandmothers.

"I remember one that was particularly unique. It had a pointed bottom and some kind of a strange design. I can't remember what it was, but it wasn't one of the usual gray corrugated or black, white, and ochre pieces."

"Was it a star pattern?" whispered Rachel.

"You know, I believe it was, and it had the four colors for mankind or the four directions painted around the opening. But you couldn't have seen it. Those pots were all destroyed before you came to the ranch. Is that the jar you replicated from Sham's adventure with the snake?"

Now Harrison was beginning to get caught up in what Rachel had been relating to him.

"Do you think the person who shot Mr. and Mrs. Thomas was looking for that jar?"

"Maybe it was someone who found it," answered Rachel. "I know Sham's mom was into Native American history, but I don't know how much she believed in all the old legends. She may not have known the significance of that particular jar. Breaking all the pottery would be a good way to disguise what was missing, wouldn't it, Harrison?"

Detective Osinski told Sham that his mom had asked for water when she was found. Maybe she wasn't asking for a drink. Maybe she was trying to tell them what the murderer had stolen. She could have been trying to say water jar."

Rachel's mind raced ahead. "Maybe Billy Dillon can get his hands on those old police reports," she said as she dialed the police station. "There must have been photographs taken at the scene."

Rachel was on hold for only a few seconds before she recognized Billy's voice.

"Hello, Rachel, how can I be of help? Have you thought of something else that might be important?" he asked hopefully.

"No, I'm sorry, but something you said about the night Sham's parents were killed rang a bell. When you looked at that file, did you see any pictures of the broken pottery?"

"Sure. They shot pictures of every room in the house from every possible angle. What are you looking for?" he asked curiously.

"Well, I'm not positive, but I think there may be one piece of the collection that might be missing. Is there any way I could get my hands on those pictures?"

"I don't see why not. I'll have to get them from the Yavapai County Sheriff. I could probably have them here this afternoon if you want to stop by. Would four o'clock be OK? I should be back in the office by then."

"That'll be just fine, Billy. Thank you. I'll tell you more about it when I get there."

Harrison was finishing the last of the peach preserves, and Rachel poured herself another cup of coffee.

"Do you remember which room the pointed jar was in when you saw it?" Rachel asked.

"It was next to a blanket chest at the foot of the bed in the master bedroom. It was propped between the corner of the chest and the footboard of the bed. I thought it was strange because it had a large stopper, and I wondered if anything was inside. What would one expect to find inside a magic water jar?"

"According to legend, salamanders and seaweed, some skim from the ocean, seashells and sand. I can't imagine how Shaman is going to find all those things. But I know why he was chosen. It's not only what's in the jar that's important. The prayers and proper procedures for procuring them must be followed exactly. It takes someone with exceptional purity to complete the ritual successfully," Rachel explained.

Then she asked, "What would someone do with the jar if they had taken it?"

Harrison thought for a moment. "If they planned on selling it, why not take some of the other rare pieces as well. No, I think if someone stole it, they had other plans. Like I said, it would be powerful medicine if you could produce water from sand. Lots of people might be willing to follow that kind of power.

"You may have found your key to this new ceremony we've been talking about," he continued. "Even if the killer was very careful to lay low after the murders, I bet he couldn't keep a thing like that to himself for too many years. Before too long, he would have been driven to use his new power to recruit other followers, and I'll bet there'd be some pretty harsh penalties if any of the society broke the code of secrecy.

"That would explain the arrow attack," Rachel interjected. "That sentry was taking his job very seriously."

"You'd be serious, too, if your head was on the line. You know, decapitation wasn't an unusual punishment for failure. That'd be a pretty potent incentive for a sentry to do his job well. Rachel, you may have a tiger by the tail here. I suggest you watch your backside very carefully. I'll be real interested in what you find out from those pictures. Mind if I stop back tonight? I'll bring a little cachana to make tea," he added in a serious tone.

Rachel knew that the root of the native cachana plant, liatris was—among sundry other medicinal uses—renowned for its ability to ward off witches and sorcerers.

"I'll be waiting with a steaming kettle," she answered just as seriously. "If you have a little extra root, I wouldn't mind a small medicine pouch to go. Clyde should get here sometime today, too. Maybe the three of us can make more sense out of this later."

After Harrison left, Rachel busied herself by visiting the local library before stopping at the clinic where she found Mike, much improved, propped up high in his adjustable bed.

"I hardly recognize you with all that color in your cheeks. For a while there I thought you had turned White," she laughingly greeted her friend.

"I'm mobile," he wrote on the large note pad, raising both arms to show the lack of intravenous needles. His throat was still grossly swollen, impairing his ability to speak, but the doctors had given their assurances that his voice would eventually return. He continued to write, "Have you found out anything?"

"I'm working on an idea," said Rachel. "Billy Dillon was here when I dropped in on you earlier. He asked about the night Shaman's parents were killed. Later, Harrison remembered a particular water jar that was in Sham's mother's pot collection. It might somehow be connected to this witchcraft ritual. Anyway, Billy is going to get the pictures of the crime scene together for me, and I'll run over this afternoon to check it out.

"I'm sorry I got you into this," she apologized.

Mike wrote laboriously, "Not your fault. Sorry, shots make me sleepy."

"You get some more rest. I have to go see Billy. I'll be back tomorrow morning."

Rachel drove the few miles to the small slit-windowed adobe building that purported to be the local Navaho police station. She found Billy waiting in his dusty little office.

"Good to see you again, Ma'am." He removed a stack of literature from one of the two chairs provided for visitors. "Sorry about the mess."

"Don't worry about it. I don't think a little dust is the most dangerous thing I've been exposed to lately."

"Yeah, you've got a point. Pollution still kills slower than arrows."

The crime-scene photographs, several layers thick, were spread out on his desk. The pictures had begun to show their age, but the patterns on the jumble of pottery shards on the floors and tabletops were still recognizable.

Something of a pottery expert in his own right, Billy studied the remains of what must have been a magnificent representation of native earthenware. Jumbled among many gray corrugated shards that might have dated as far back as 700 A.D., polished black-and-red remains from the Santa Clara and San Ildefonso pueblos were easily recognizable.

"Look at that." Billy pointed to a large piece of clay that represented nearly a full half of an extremely fine black-on-white example of work produced in the Kayenta area around 1200 A.D.

Rachel mourned the museum-quality shard lying at the tip of Billy's fingernail. She was overwhelmed at the magnitude of the destruction of this important collection. How could anyone have destroyed these magnificent examples of Native American art?

"Billy, I think the Thomases may have been killed because of a special piece of pottery in Mrs. Thomas's collection. I'm looking for any pieces in these photographs that match a particular design, but I didn't realize there would be so many. Is there any chance I could take these back to the lodge?" Rachel asked.

"I guess so," said Billy. "I don't think anyone will lose any sleep over photographs of a forty-year-old crime scene. Just drop them off before you head back to the ranch. I can't imagine a piece of pottery that would outshine some of those in these photographs."

"Sure thing," promised Rachel, as she stacked the photos back into their box and prepared to leave. "If I'm right, the pot I'm looking for is the mother of all pots."

Walking her to the door, Billy added, "You know, Detective Osinski always thought the murders had something to do with that mess of broken pottery, but there was no full inventory of the pieces anywhere. Mrs. Thomas didn't bother insuring them, and she was always moving them around or adding new ones. Osinski never really bought the transient drug users theory, but he never got a break in the case. If you find anything, I'd sure like to solve that one for him. He taught me a lot. He was a good cop," Billy praised the now-deceased detective. "Maybe you better take this magnifying glass along. We might as well be thorough."

"Well, if it's not in any of these pictures, it's most probable that someone stole it. I don't think Sham's mom would have gotten rid of such a prize. I'll call you as soon as I finish with the pictures.

CHAPTER XXX

Looking for The Pieces

Rachel, with the pictures of the murder scene, headed back to the lodge, hoping that Clyde would be waiting for her there.

"Excuse me; has Clyde White Antelope checked in yet?" Rachel inquired of the Navaho woman perched on a stool behind the small check-in counter.

The desk clerk closed her book, keeping it in one hand, a finger securing the page where she had left off reading, and peered around the cheap brochures that were displayed in front of the desk.

"I know there's a message here somewhere." The disembodied words floated up to Rachel from the now invisible clerk who had bent down and, with her one free hand, was rifling through a mess of papers spread haphazardly across the counter shelf.

While the clerk continued her groping explorations, Rachel tapped her foot and restrained herself from going behind the counter to look. Instead, she took note of the jewelry, artifacts and books available for sale in the gift shop portion of the room.

"Here it is," the clerk finally said. With a smile of triumph, she produced a note clutched in the hand not holding the novel, as though she had at last discovered a long-lost treasure. Rachel stopped tapping her foot. She accepted the note and excitedly read, I'm here and I'm hungry. Where are you? Call me. Clyde

There was no answer when she phoned his room, so she headed for the cafeteria. Clyde was the only patron. He was sitting in a booth beneath one of the large Navaho rugs that decorated the walls throughout the dining area.

Along with the rugs, there were antique bows and arrows and other tools of war sprinkled intermittently among the peace pipes and buckskin frocks of long ago. Each one dangled a price tag like a fishing lure. Rachel stopped briefly at the booth.

"Clyde, I'm so glad you're here. Wait until I tell you what's been happening. First I have to get something to eat. My stomach is so empty it thinks my throat's been cut. What are you eating?"

"Try the hominy stew and baked squash blossoms," he suggested.

"Is the hominy made with chamisa or juniper ash?" Rachel asked.

"Juniper," Clyde said. "It doesn't have the blue-green color of chamisa. Besides, this is Navaho country now. You're not likely to find much Hopi 'soul food' on the menu. But I've arranged for blue marbles for breakfast. Want to join me."

"Thanks, but no thanks. I just have coffee in the morning."

Rachel moved to the food service area and pushed her tray along the counter. She ordered the same meal as Clyde's, plus an order of sweet corn pudding, and carried her tray back to his booth. She unloaded the tray, talking all the while.

"Was everything all right with Zoe? Did she seem okay to you?"

"Everything is fine at the ranch," Clyde assured her. Zoe is none the worse for wear, and Hyacinth is staying close by. Zoe has some strange stories to tell, but she really seems to be just fine."

"Thanks for checking on her."

Clyde looked around the room. One couple had taken a table some distance away. The booths on either side of them were still empty. His face took on a troubled expression.

"Now, tell me how Mike got shot."

Between mouthfuls, Rachel brought him up to date on her activities. "We were up near Martini Cave, checking out a tip about a ceremony being held there. Before we could get close enough to see anything, someone shot Mike in the throat with an arrow. They must have had sentries posted. Mike is recovering well."

"Something new has been thrown into the mix," Rachel continued. "Were you very familiar with the Thomas pot collection, Clyde?" she asked.

"I remember it was all over the place. I was always scared to death that I'd break one," he answered.

Rachel broached her theory on burglary, connected to murder, connected to witchcraft. She explained, "I have some photographs of the ranch right after Sham's mom and dad were killed. I'm looking for a particular design in the mess of shattered pottery. I think someone stole that jar, and Sham's parent's just happened to walk in at the wrong time. I'm not quite sure how the pot fits in yet, but I believe whoever stole it is involved in this witchcraft thing today. Do you remember a large, pointed jar with a star-burst design?" Clyde mulled this over.

"It sounds vaguely familiar, but I'm not really sure. There were so many of them. Do you have the photographs here?"

"Yes, I got them from Billy Dillon. They're in my room."

"After we eat, we'll go back to your room, and I'll help you with the pictures. You can draw me a sketch. If there's no trace of the jar, then you may be right. I do know that Sham's mom would never get rid of any piece of her collection on purpose." Rachel gulped her food and they returned to her room. She put the photographs on the night table and sat down to draw a quick sketch of the jar.

"We can divide them up. Billy loaned me a magnifying glass, too."

Before they could get started, Harrison was knocking on the door. Rachel let him in and everyone said their yat ta hehs before Harrison produced his cachana tea and a small decorated medicine pouch that he had prepared especially for Rachel.

"Who ever heard of a witch's brew in a thermos?" Rachel laughed.

"That's because it's a no-witches brew," said Harrison. "I added a few other items along with the cachana root in your medicine pouch. You don't need to know what they are. Just keep it with you at all times." With a little flourish Harrison handed the pouch to Rachel. They shared the tea while Rachel once again replicated the design of the elusive jar. Harrison was soon put to work with another copy of the sketch and his own stack of photos.

"There must be over two hundred pictures here," he groaned. "They sure didn't miss anything when they covered that crime scene."

As they poured over the aged photographs, Rachel was aware of how little the ranch had changed since the death of Sham's parents.

The antique rugs and hand-woven blankets still decorated the master bedroom, as well as the rest of the ranch. The heavy oak and cedar furnishings were still abundant throughout the house, blending in with the few contemporary pieces that she had managed to add without upsetting the basic western motif. Rachel remarked how much she would have liked to have known the woman who left this place before her time.

"Your own parents died rather tragically, too," she addressed Clyde. She touched his arm as she remembered how broken up he had been when he got the news of his father's suicide, and added, "These shattered pieces of that beautiful collection are like our hearts when we lose someone we love." Clyde nodded and covered her hand with his. To acknowledge the comforting touch Rachel said,

"Yes, our family was never the same after Mom broke her neck in that fall. She was practically born on a horse, so the last thing we'd expect was for her to be thrown. My dad never got over it. He walked around in a daze most of the time after that. It wasn't until his suicide that I learned he blamed himself for her death." Rachel remembered the strange suicide note.

"Did you have any idea what he meant about his having sacrificed everyone?"

"I never understood any of it. It was like he was talking in parables," Clyde answered. "He wrote a lot of stuff about the final retribution and burning in the great pit. I think he had pretty much just lost it by then. He'd outlived everyone in the family but me. All four of my sisters were gone, and he was alone on that ranch he finally bought. He had even buried his own grandchildren. I couldn't get him to come to New Mexico. Whenever I approached him on the subject, he just said he couldn't leave his land after all he'd sacrificed for it." The conversation ebbed as they combed every photograph, finding no evidence of a star-shaped design in any of them.

"Well, folks," Harrison said, "I think we have a real mystery here. I'd sure appreciate it if you'd keep me posted on developments. It's time for me to call it a night. If I can be of any help, just call."

"Thanks Harrison, we'll do that. I'm ready to pack it in, too," Rachel said. "I think we can be pretty sure the pot is missing. It is getting late, and I still want to browse through a couple of books before I fall asleep. I'll meet you for breakfast, Clyde. We can check on Mike before time to meet Shaman. We need to arrange for three horses in the morning, and Mike said we can use his land rover as long as we need it. There's enough blood in it right now to puke a buzzard off a gut wagon, so I'll have to get it cleaned up."

"Sounds like you've picked up another one of Mike's favorite phrases," Harrison commented. "I'll be happy to have it cleaned up for you, and I'll take care of the horses, too," he offered. "Just tell me where you want them, and when."

"Great, I'll give you the particulars on the way out," said Clyde. "Will two o'clock be Okay, Rachel?"

"That sounds great. I'd like to be there before dark." Rachel thought of her last foray into a dark canyon and shuddered. "Good night, both of you."

CHAPTER XXXI

Connecting The Pieces

Alone in her room, Rachel settled down to the books. In the second volume she found a definite reference to witchcraft. It seemed there were four degrees of witches. To avoid a long-suffering afterlife, the first three could atone for their evil deeds by sacrificing their harvests or personal belongings before they died. The fourth, however, had to sacrifice the lives of their families to sustain their own lives; and these witches, or sorcerers—known to the Hopi as Powaqa—would burn after death until all seven worlds are completed. According to this formula, a girl sacrifice insured four additional years of life to the witch, and a boy only two.

Hadn't Clyde just mentioned outliving all four of his sisters? He had also performed the Ya Ya ceremony back in the early 2000s. Rachel did a little mental arithmetic. Four times four, plus the mother, is twenty. Adding two for dear old dad, she came up with twenty-two years. Just when had they attended that ceremony in Chaco Canyon? To the best of her recollection, it was three or four years after she and Sham were married.

The numbers were off by about ten years, and what about the magic water jar? Clyde had been at a ceremony when Sham's parents were murdered, and she was more certain than ever that the two mysteries were somehow tied together.

"I can't believe what I was just thinking," she announced to the empty room. Fragmented thoughts chased each other around her mental track until she finally slept for a couple of hours.

She was already up and dressed when Clyde knocked on her door at 6:00 a.m. Her stomach felt queasy, probably from lack of sleep, so she settled for coffee while Clyde had his breakfast of blue marbles.

This was not a dish that Rachel had ever been very fond of. It was a traditional Hopi dish of marble-sized dough balls made from blue cornmeal, flavored with chamisa ash and a spoonful of sugar, served with dried onions and salt-pork.

"Did you learn anything more from your books last night?" Clyde asked, between mouthfuls.

"A little," she replied. "One of them had a chapter on witches, with pertinent information on degrees of evil and longevity. You know, Clyde, these stories have been around me all my life and never registered until now. It surprises me how much I thought I knew about Indian cultures, only to discover that I was picking and choosing just the information that I found believable. What I've been reading is nothing new. I've read it all before. But now I'm seeing it from a different perspective."

Rachel continued, "Universal harmony as a ceremonial goal was easy to accept. It's comforting. I readily entertained the concept. Sorcery and witches were only stories; counterpoints to emphasize the need for religious diligence. Now I realize that men with darkness in their hearts can channel the power of the communal will to forces that threaten the annihilation of mankind. We either grow as a community, or we perish."

"I guess we all dissemble to some extent," said Clyde. "The tribes incorporate other religions into their own value systems. We're constantly discarding old kachinas that have lost their beneficial powers in favor of a new one that might have more going for it. New rituals spring up all the time.

"Today, nearly all of the Native American populations have accepted Christianity in some form, but many so-called converts still do their ceremonial dances on the hard-packed chapel floors.

"Incredulity can be pretty hard to overcome for all of us," he continued. "Though Native Americans are more likely than some to find all religions acceptable as part of the whole, we also pick and choose among the prevailing beliefs of a new religion."

Rachel sipped her coffee and decided to do some additional research.

"Clyde, would you mind going alone to check on Mike? There's someone I'd like to talk to. I can meet you back here by noon."

"No problem. Anyone I know?"

"His name is John Stetson. He's the grandson of one of my archaeology professors. He used to keep some pretty accurate records of all the local families on the Hopi reservation. Maybe he can give us a lead. His ranch is quite a way out, but if I leave now, I think I can be back in time. I'll need the land rover. Here are the keys to the truck."

Rachel stood up so fast that she nearly collided with the man rising from the next booth.

Sorry," she muttered.

"No harm done," the stranger forgave her then tipped his silver-banded cowboy hat.

"Are you sure you'll be all right by yourself?" Clyde asked. "You seem a little nervous. I'll be happy to go with you."

"No thanks, Clyde. I'd much prefer it if you'd visit Mike for me. I'll be fine."

She waved a quick goodbye and went in search of Mike's vehicle. She found it—minus any sign of the crusty brown stains—in front of the lodge. The keys were in the ignition. She knew there was no danger that the vehicle could be stolen. Harrison would certainly have left someone to watch over it. She spotted the sentry lounging against the building and thanked him with a wave. He gave a short salute and sauntered toward the corral.

Rachel began her drive to John Stetson's and called him on the cellular phone to make sure he'd be expecting her. He seemed delighted that she was on her way. Arriving some time later, she found John waiting for her at the door. She enjoyed the welcome in his laughing brown eyes as he encircled her in his thin arms. Rachel envied John's metabolic rate. She knew how much he loved to eat.

"It's so good to see you, Rachel. It's been such a long time. What have you been doing with yourself?" John welcomed her, ushering her into the familiar office.

She seated herself in a large leather chair. In front of her was a hand-hewn cedar table bearing a tray of coffee and Indian cake. The cake, made from a mixture of cornmeal, molasses, and butter, was a staple at John's house. Rachel couldn't remember ever visiting here without facing a platter piled to overflowing with Indian cake.

"I see you haven't lost your sweet tooth, John," she kidded him.

"I hope I never do. It seems I'm always losing other bits and pieces as the years go by. Last year it was the old gall bladder. The year before that, my kidney transplant just up and quit on me. Luckily, I was already having one cloned as a backup, and it was ready to install. Hopefully, I won't have to give up the simple pleasure of eating. To what do I owe this unexpected visit?"

I'd like your help on the birth and death records of some Hopi families. Your files are probably more accurate than the ones I could get from the county records, and besides, I like your Indian cake," she said, and helped herself to refreshments. "I'm only interested in the records since 2010."

"Just the last thirty-eight years?" John laughed. "Let me make sure this computer knows you're friendly. It won't talk to just anyone. It'll only take a minute. Are these all reservation Hopi?"

"I didn't know you kept records of any others." If John's files would actually let her track some of the Hopi who did not live on the reservation, Rachel couldn't believe her good fortune.

"I think my dad finally located a source on every family that had any ties with the reservation over the last half century," John responded. "Some of the people are spread all over hell and half of Georgia by now, but I usually get at least a yearly update from some surviving family member."

"Your dad always did keep precise records. I really miss him."

"So do I," John said softly. "His passing was a great loss to many. The Hopi were his passion."

"I remember the first time I heard him lecture," Rachel said. "What stood out was how this very small race of people managed to outlast several hundreds of years of contact with foreign influences."

"That was one of his favorite subjects," John interjected. "They've not been able to remain totally uncontaminated, of course, but there are some who still live mostly by the old ways, and many more who retain some ties to the old belief system. I marvel at their tenacity."

"I know what you mean." Rachel agreed. "Since you have them available, I'd appreciate the lists of all the families."

While John fed the retrieval codes into his computer, they chatted for a few moments about their shared respect for the Hopi.

"Just say one, two, three," John instructed Rachel.

Rachel did as she was told, and John entered her voice identification pattern into the computer.

"Here you are, my dear. The machine is bursting with information and anxious to enlighten you. Ask to your heart's content. I'll leave you alone for now. Call if you need anything." John left the room, closing the door behind him, and Rachel began to research the statistics on file in his computer.

Remembering last night's conversation, she started with Clyde's family. Since they did not live on the reservation, Rachel had not expected to find them in John's files. She had no idea these records would be so complete.

Sure enough, Clyde's sisters were each listed. The first two had died four years apart, but there were eight years separating the death of the second sister and the demise of the third, and ten years before the last. Continuing the research on Clyde's family, she found the unsettling records of several of his nephews and a niece. One girl and three boys had passed away during those longer spans between the deaths of his sisters. By her arithmetic, that would exactly fill the time discrepancies which, like a smorgasbord, had fed her quilt for entertaining the thought of Clyde as a suspect.

John's records were listed by clan. Much of her work had been simplified by his method of storage and retrieval. She could ask the computer to recite or display a written family history including intermarriages, propensity for assimilation, and just which rituals could be claimed by that particular clan. After two hours of diligent research, Rachel was pretty sure she'd covered the necessary ground.

She stuffed her notes into her bag and went in search of John. She discovered him talking to a stranger in the driveway. The man looked somewhat familiar, but she couldn't quite identify him.

"Thank you, John," she interrupted. "I'm sorry I have to rush, but I promise to come back soon."

"Try to make it in this decade," John said. The stranger tipped his hat to Rachel. As she backed up, Rachel remembered where she had seen this man before. He had tipped his silver-banded hat the same way at the restaurant when she nearly ran over him this morning. She hesitated for a moment. The man nodded good-bye to John and got into the jeep parked next to her and backed down the drive.

"Did you forget something?" John startled her at the driver's window.

"No, I was just trying to remember where I knew your friend from. I think I recognize him, but I can't place his name."

"He's really not a friend, just someone who was asking directions. He took a wrong turn about five miles back. Sorry I can't help you with a name. I didn't bother to ask. I meant what I said about coming back soon."

"So did I," said Rachel. Thanks, again."

She headed back toward the Thunderbird Lodge, looking in her rear-view mirror every few minutes. Could it have been just a coincidence, running into the same stranger twice in one morning? Why not? After all, this was reservation land. Many of the roads were still unmarked trails leading to sparsely populated areas. The people who lived here knew where they were going. They felt no compulsion to announce their homes to strangers. The next time she glanced in the mirror, Rachel asked aloud,

"Mirror, Mirror, on the wall, who's the most paranoid of them all?"

Suddenly, the mirror was filled with a jeep approaching very fast. By its own volition, her foot pressed the accelerator to the floor. Mike's car rapidly reached its maximum speed. Only inches separated the two vehicles.

Her mirror now reflected the menacing leer plastered across the driver's face partially obscured beneath the large, silver-banded hat. Rachel momentarily removed one hand from the steering wheel and clutched her new medicine bag. She pressed her foot hard to the floorboard. Her peripheral vision registered a small herd of sheep entering the road on her right. There was barely time to swerve left of the bleating animals, and she missed an oncoming transport by a hair's breadth.

The trailing jeep was not so lucky. The huge transport was unable to avoid making contact with the second vehicle.

The leer that had filled her mirror a moment before became a scream of terror as the jeep, scattering bleating sheep, careened back across the pavement. The car rolled over and finally rested a good distance beyond the highway.

Rachel backed her own vehicle up to the site of the accident. The transport driver was already racing toward the overturned jeep. Luckily for him, the car exploded in a deadly fireball several seconds before he could reach it. There was little left of the blackened wreck, but the now familiar hat lay near the road.

As the stunned long-hauler watched in amazement, Rachel, still shaking, left the scene. What should she do now? After this close encounter with a speeding maniac and what she'd just learned from John's files, she trusted no one. She dialed the lodge and asked for Clyde.

"Hello, Clyde. How's Mike doing?" she questioned him in as calm a voice as she could muster.

"He's much improved. The doctors expect a full recovery. He won't be talking for a while, but he wrote a note for you. It reads, 'Watch your back'."

Rachel shivered at the aptness of Mike's warning. That was twice she'd heard that phrase in the past few hours.

"I'm glad that he's feeling better," she managed. "Listen, it's nearly twelve now, and I'm closer to Keet Seel than I am to the lodge. Wait for me there. Shaman and I will meet you tomorrow morning."

"Rachel, what's wrong?" asked Clyde, his voice full of concern. "I worry about you going alone."

"Nothing's wrong. It's just easier this way, and I'd like a little time alone with Shaman. Surely you understand. It's not that I don't appreciate everything you've done. Believe me. Just be patient, and we'll see you in the morning."

"It sounds like I don't have much choice." Clyde sounded more than a little irritated. "Harrison called, and he's arranged for the horses. They'll be waiting where you left your jeep. Take care, Rachel." The irritation had quickly passed, and with these words, his voice expressed only concern.

Rachel dialed the ranch but got no answer. The birth and death references relating to Clyde's family were not the only alarming statistics she had come across in John's files. She had just acquired some information concerning Pappy Coyote's family that was very disturbing, as well.

Why doesn't Hyacinth answer the phone? After twenty rings Rachel hung up and dialed the lodge again.

"Hello, this is Rachel Thomas. Are there any messages for me?"

"Wait just a moment. I'll check." Rachel could hear the clerk rummaging through the ever present stack of papers that never seemed to get filed in any order. It was a miracle anyone ever got a message.

"Just one, would you like me to read it?"

"Yes, please," Rachel said anxiously.

"We'll wait at Kawestima until morning." It's signed, Zoe. That's all there is. Will there be anything else, ma'am?"

"Yes, please ring Clyde White Antelope's room for me."

After a moment the desk clerk came back on the line.

"I'm sorry, ma'am. There's no answer."

Rachel hung up without even a thank you. Who had written that note? Zoe wouldn't have used the Hopi name for Betatakin. Why did no one answer at the ranch? Should she go straight to Betatakin or find Shaman first? The questions swirled in her head until her need to be with Shaman won out. The decision made, she once again pressed the accelerator to the floor and headed for Keet Seel.

The horses were corralled as promised, enabling her to get to the ruins much faster than her last journey. When she arrived, Shaman was nowhere to be seen. She rested for a moment in the keyhole-shaped kiva. As she tried to pull her thoughts together, the sipapu hole began to widen. Rachel inched closer. It was large enough to enter, but she had no idea how far the drop would be to the bottom.

Remembering Zoe's description of her fall into the first sipapu hole, Rachel decided to chance it. She crawled backward into the hole and was surprised to find a ladder rung beneath her foot. As she reached the bottom of the ladder, the hole above began to seal itself. Buried beneath the ruins, Rachel experienced darkness as absolute as pre-creation. The stalking presence of panic slithered near.

"Get a grip, Rachel," she chastised her cringing child-self. "You're here for a reason. That sipapu hole invited you in, so relax and see what develops." With her inner child properly disciplined, her heart rate slowly returned to normal.

"Hello, Rachel," said a soft voice. "Don't be frightened. Close your eyes and let your inner eye guide you. I will accompany you part of the way to your destination."

Relieved to hear the sound of another voice, Rachel did as she was told. Alo took Rachel's hand, and as they entered and exited several caverns, the forbidding blackness progressively gave way to gloomy shadows and finally to complete visibility. Beside her was an Indian woman who perfectly matched the description Zoe had given.

"Are you Alo?" inquired Rachel.

"I am to Zoe," the stranger replied in the same soft voice as before. "You and I met once before under different circumstances. Do you remember?" Rachel recognized the turquoise eyes of her flashlight benefactress of many years ago.

"Yes, I remember," she said. "Do you know how many times I've thanked you for that flashlight?"

"Yes, I do, and you are very welcome. It was the least I could do for Shaman and his bride."

"Are you the spirit of Shaman's mother?" Rachel ventured.

"She, and many who preceded her, and some who will follow," answered her new companion. "There is continuity to all things. Each particle of energy is constantly evolving, and each contains the substance of the whole."

"And Zoe holds the future, doesn't she?"

"It is a burden she has earned," Alo replied. "The people are again losing their spiritual awareness, and unless they wake up soon, the time of the Fifth World is very near. Today's physical world is gasping on its deathbed. Zoe may be its last hope, and you and Shaman must be her armor against evil. Wait here by this boulder and Shaman will join you soon."

Before Rachel could ask anything more, the spirit vanished. Rachel sat and contemplated the skeletal remains that lay trapped beneath the boulder beside her.

Chapter XXXII

Purification

Shaman knelt in the shallow eddies at the edge of the underground sea. Paying no heed to the water lapping over his naked body, he waited for a sign. The sign came in the form of a vision.

In his vision, Sham could see the water jar planted in the earth. From the jar poured a crystal stream that flowed by ancient ruins. A clear lake, surrounded by trees and plants rippled in the bright sunlight. Animals were abundant. From the middle of the ruins, Zoe peered into the far distance, toward great cities on the horizon. There, towers filled with laughing people spiraled toward a sunny sky that had conquered the world of pollution.

Sensing that the time was right, Shaman planted the paho in the sand of the receding water. While repeating the necessary prayers, he scraped with the sacred eagle's wingtip to obtain a few small salamanders and placed them in the jar. He finished the ritual collection of all the required items. Then it was time to begin his return to Keet Seel.

He retrieved his clothes after once again swimming past the flowstone, holding the water jar well above the water.

Shaman was surprised to find Rachel waiting in the cavern where the skeleton still lay entrapped beneath the boulder. They embraced for several moments and drew comfort from one another in this strange underground world. Rachel was the first to speak.

"Someone knows we're witch-hunting, Shaman. They're holding Zoe at Betatakin. They left a message for me at the lodge."

"That must be what Clawing Bear was trying to warn me about." Shaman ran his hand through his hair and paced back and forth, never letting the jar out of his grasp.

Hardly believing her own ears, Rachel relayed her own fears.

"Shaman, I think Clyde may be a witch. Pappy could be one, too. I've learned a lot in the past two days. The witch we're seeking might be either one or both of them." She explained all that had occurred at Canyon de Chelly, and Shaman listened intently.

With a new urgency, he turned to the silent skeleton. Sham spoke as though to an old acquaintance.

"Where were you planning on burying this jar, my friend?"

Momentarily forgetting her own recent encounter with a spirit of her acquaintance, Rachel was perplexed with Sham's attempt to converse with this inert pile of bones. Before she could utter a word, the Hisatsinom apparition once again appeared.

"You called," it merely stated as Rachel stared, dumbfounded.

"Yes, I called." Sham spoke more curtly than intended, and hastened to explain, "I need to get this jar planted so we can find our granddaughter. Can you help us access the opening to Talastima, respectfully using the Hopi name for Keet Seel?"

"That won't be necessary," replied the apparition. "I was only a short distance from my destination when this catastrophe of a rock struck me down. Return to the cavern directly beneath the kiva. There, near the wall, you will find a receptacle already dug. This is the place where you must plant the jar. When you have done this, a pure stream of life-giving water will begin to flow downhill. You can follow it until you reach Kawestima—I'm afraid I was eaves-dropping, bad habits are hard to break. You will approach from the caverns at the rear. I believe you know the ones. Now go quickly, and good luck." Again the apparition disappeared. As they retraced their steps to plant the water jar, Rachel recounted her theory that the murders of Sham's parents were directly related to the theft of the pottery.

"That's what my skeletal friend must have been referring to when he asked if I recognized the jar," said Sham. "Of course, I remember—now that you mention it. That was the jar that sat at the foot of their bed. Mom kept it cradled in antique blankets next to her big cedar chest. It was one of her favorite pieces. I guess someone better versed in Indian rituals could have known the importance of that particular jar. I'm pretty sure Mom didn't."

Sham found the hole, more like a small well, near the wall of the cavern, and placed the jar in it. Immediately, the well filled with water, and a small stream began to meander downhill. They turned and followed the stream through a maze of connecting caverns.

The caves spiraled down for some distance. In one of the lower caves, Sham and Rachel were unprepared for the horror confronting them when they stumbled upon a jumble of mutilated bodies strewn about haphazardly.

These corpses were not long-dead skeletons or mummified remains of cherished loved ones of ancient peoples. These were recently murdered victims in different stages of decomposition.

The bones of worm-eaten skeletons were scattered everywhere. Sham and Rachel passed one headless carcass that moved and rumbled with the innervating explosions of internal gases.

The guiding stream flowed more quickly now. Mapping its stream-bed ever wider, it parted the deceased, washing them to either side.

Shaman grabbed Rachel's hand and pulled her along quickly, leaving the dead to the dark cave. They raced through several more caverns before resting briefly in the cavern where Rachel had landed after falling behind the pictograph-covered boulder. This cave was lower than those beyond, and soon the stream began to puddle. They made their way toward the ominous kiva through which Rachel had escaped on their previous trip. They heard the sounds of voices and stopped short of entering the kiva.

Chapter XXXIII

Revelation

Zoe was perched on the raised kiva bench that encircled the room. She held tightly to Hyacinth's hand.

"I'm sorry, Zoe. I didn't know," Hyacinth wept. "I'm sure your grandparents will come soon. Don't be frightened."

In the center of the room, next to several jars with perforated hide coverings, Pappy and Clyde were having a heated discussion.

"I will not be a party to this," Clyde argued.

"Of course you will," Pappy sneered. "You've been a part of it for over thirty years. Did you really think you were that good a lawyer? Your power has always come from the Ya Ya. Your father knew it. He was willing to sacrifice everyone for you."

"What do you mean?"

"Didn't you read his suicide note? What did you think he meant? Your mother was the first. She shouldn't have meddled. She happened to come into the potting shed when I was taking the magic water jar out of hiding. That jar could bring water back to the lands of our ancestors. She recognized it as part of the Thomas collection. I went through hell to get that jar, and she broke it before I could bring the people home," Pappy snapped.

"You killed the Thomases?" Clyde couldn't believe what he was hearing.

Pappy spoke without emotion, "The first time I saw it in the bedroom I knew it was the magic water jar that belonged to our people. With that jar, I could rebuild our homeland in the place of our ancestors, but I knew only the snake ceremony. That wouldn't give me enough power to stand against the Whites and Navahos."

Clyde saw the fanaticism in Pappy's eyes and wondered how he had been so blind to it all these years.

"You killed my mother, too?"

"I had to. Just when I had the power of the Ya Ya at my fingertips, she was going to ruin everything."

"But you're no priest. You don't know the ritual for the Ya Ya."

"I got most of it from watching you the first time you gave that little demonstration for your father."

"But we were alone," Clyde insisted. "You didn't show up until we were nearly finished. You were looking for a stallion that had bolted his pen."

"He didn't get out by accident. I followed you that night and watched you prepare for the Ya Ya. I had the stallion tethered nearby, just in case. If that loose rock hadn't given me away, you would never have known I was there. Too bad you didn't get to finish the ceremony."

"That's right. You couldn't use the ceremony. So why kill the Thomases?"

"How could I know you would wait years to perform the Ya Ya again? With the magic water jar and the power of the Ya Ya, I could lead my people home."

Pappy's eyes flashed with the light of the true zealot, willing to do anything, even kill, to reclaim the place of his ancestors and rejuvenate the wasted mesas that surrounded the ancient cliff dwellings.

"When your father came to me and asked me to take part in your ritual, I showed him how we could get others to join us. He was very angry about the Thomases, but he wanted you to use the power of the Ya Ya. He told no one what I had done. We used the jar to recruit the others for the ceremony at Chaco Canyon. No one connected it to the Thomases."

"You killed Sham's parents for a jar!" Clyde was still stunned by Pappy's revelations.

"It wasn't just any jar, and they weren't supposed to be there. When they came in, I was just leaving. The gun was on the hall rack. I panicked and grabbed the gun. I had no choice."

Pappy continued, "I thought they both died instantly, but I guess the old woman must have heard me smashing the pot collection to cover the disappearance of the one I took. Lucky for me, she died before telling anyone. I was able to rejoin the other men as they emerged from the kiva.

"Unfortunately," continued Pappy, "after Chaco Canyon, your mother found the jar. She knew that it was part of the Thomas collection. The fool was on her way to the police when I caught up with her. She broke the damn thing before I could retrieve it. I couldn't let her betray us, even though she was my cousin.

"Without the jar, I had to forget about returning to the place of our ancestors, but the lure of the Ya Ya was too strong. I couldn't give that up, too, and now I didn't need you.

"Once I crossed the line by killing your mother, I had no choice. I had entered the lowest realm of the two-heart. My life now depended on sacrificing my family. I convinced your father that it was your life on the line because you were the one who revived the Ya Ya. You must have thought your family had some very bad luck."

"What do you mean?" Clyde was afraid to ask, but he had to know. "Are you saying mother wasn't the only one? There was never anything suspicious about any of my family's deaths. By today's mortality standards, most of them weren't even that young."

"That was a help." Pappy grinned maniacally. "Your father was easy. He was full of guilt because he was the one who had pushed you to get the knowledge of the Ya Ya. All the time your father thought his dear ones were being sacrificed for you. It never dawned on him that they were my family, too. For your sake, he kept his silence. I finally convinced him that only his own death could add extra years to your life. He was loyal to the end. He even wrote a suicide note so it'd look like he killed himself."

While making this confession, Pappy was opening the coverings on the jars. After he unfastened the last one, he kicked each jar over before running to the notched hand-holds leading from the kiva.

"Good-bye," he called over his shoulder. "Give my best to our family." With that, he disappeared through the kiva opening and closed it from above with a large stone. A stunned Clyde stared as dozens of snakes began to slither their way out of the jars that had been toppled.

Before talking to Rachel four days ago, Clyde had no inkling that the Ya Ya had been subverted. He knew he was a good lawyer, and as he saw it, the added power derived from the Ya Ya was no more than his rightful inheritance. He had never performed the ceremony with the intent of personal gain. He did know that it had given him special insights, which he had not been above employing in his everyday activities.

It was hard to believe that Pappy was the witch they were looking for, and that his father had been a party to the sad state of affairs that afflicted this world. Knowingly or not, so had he.

As Clyde dealt with his new insight, Shaman and Rachel rushed into the kiva from the adjoining cavern, only to be stopped short by the numerous reptiles crawling in all directions.

"Clyde," yelled Shaman. "We heard. Snap out of it. Can you reach us?"

Clyde shook his head, peered at them, and finally focused on the surrounding snakes.

"Stop, don't move," he whispered. "Everyone do exactly as I do."

Clyde sat where he was and closed his eyes, then began the chant of the snake ceremony. The other four mimicked Clyde exactly. Closing their eyes and remaining perfectly still, they echoed the cadence of the ritual sound.

The snakes began to approach the chanting figures. First one singer, then another felt the undulating motion of the reptiles as they investigated these strange people sitting like statues in their midst. No one moved, and all continued the hypnotic chant until Clyde gave them new instructions.

"Open your eyes. If there are any snakes on you, do not disturb them." They all opened their eyes but continued the chant. Each of them had at least one snake curled in a lap. Zoe was practically covered. She sat deathly still under more than a dozen sleeping reptiles.

Zoe took one peek and quickly closed her eyes again. She could stand the weight of the snakes, but she did not want to have to look at them.

Clyde could see that the kiva opening was closed off to them. He removed the one snake from his body by holding it gently behind the head. Stroking it as he moved, he replaced it in one of the empty jars.

"We will have to leave the way you came in," he announced to the others. Sit still until I can remove these napping fellows from your laps. At least we can be pretty sure that all of us are somewhat trustworthy. We've each been selected by at least one of these viper judges. Zoe, you have so many snakes on you because they trust you. They've chosen you as their friend. Just be still a minute longer and we'll get you uncovered."

Clyde and Shaman efficiently dealt with the remaining snakes, returning them to their uncovered jars.

"They should be able to find their way back home when they wake up," said Clyde.

Retracing the path followed by Shaman and Rachel on their journey from Keet Seel, the little party found that the puddle in the lower caverns had become a small lake.

They stopped to rest in one of the higher caves, and Rachel turned to Clyde. "I owe you an apology, Clyde. When I was at John Stetson's this morning, I checked his computer records and found the dates of the deaths of the members of your family. I'm sorry I jumped to conclusions."

"That's why you left me at the lodge this morning?"

"Only partly: As I was leaving John's place, I saw a man who had been at the restaurant when we had breakfast together. You might remember. I almost ran over him as I was getting up to leave. He was wearing a hat with a silver band."

"I vaguely recall him," offered Clyde.

"He followed me from John's. After we'd gone a few miles, he tried to run me off the road. I barely missed a head-on collision with a large transport. I'm afraid my pursuer wasn't so lucky. His vehicle rolled and burned. It must have been running on propane. Some of the old models still use it.

"After that incident, I was afraid to pick you up before seeing Sham. When you and I finished talking, I got my messages from the lodge. After I found out Zoe had been taken to Betatakin, I went straight to Sham."

"Well, I don't blame you, Rachel. Under the circumstances, I must have looked pretty guilty," Clyde acknowledged. "I guess, in some ways, I am. I never really did it intentionally, but what's that old saying Mike is always using?"

"The road to hell is paved with good intentions?" quoted Rachel.

"Yeah, that's the one."

"How did you get to the kiva so quickly?" she asked.

"I was worried after your call. I checked the desk to see if you had received any messages. The desk clerk told me about the message from Zoe. I didn't know if you were still on your way to Keet Seel, or if you'd go directly to Betatakin, but I figured you'd get here sooner or later. When I got here, Pappy met me at the Great Cave and led me to the kiva. On the way, he started explaining some of how he had been directing the power of the Ya Ya. You heard the rest inside the kiva.

"Rachel, when you started asking questions about witches, he thought you might know something. Then he saw your replica of the magic water jar. After his arrow missed its mark, you went through John Stetson's records, and the old rogue thought you might have figured out the relationship between the deaths of Sham's parents and the water jar.

"The man who followed you from John's was probably one of Pappy's acolytes. You must have a guardian angel, or Harrison made you one powerful medicine bag. When Silver Hat didn't get the job done, Pappy decided to use Zoe as a hostage. Pappy knew you would bring Sham, and he expected him to have the new water jar. He thought he might still have a chance to reclaim the Hisatsinom lands.

"When I showed up alone, he was furious. I told him you were on your way to Keet Seal, that I had gotten the message and came in your place. I told him I left a note for you to meet me back at the ranch."

Rachel shivered. "I guess that's why he didn't wait until morning to dispose of Zoe. He's probably rushing back to ambush us at the ranch."

CHAPTER XXXIV

Resolution

Pappy Coyote had not returned to the ranch. Along with the other Ya Ya apostles, he was searching the ruins of Keet Seel. Because Rachel's horse and the spare mount were waiting patiently for their riders to return, Pappy was expecting to find Shaman and Rachel somewhere in the vicinity.

If Rachel could see the hunters now, she would sadly have recognized her old friend, John Stetson. His skeletal frame darted among the angry searchers who, under the direction of a frantic Pappy Coyote, were combing the rooms of Keet Seel.

After all the years that it had taken for him to establish himself as a priest of the Ya Ya, Pappy Coyote had no intention of letting Shaman and Rachel Thomas upset his future.

For years Clyde's father had been the only obstacle to Pappy's total control of the Ya Ya initiates. With the death of his only deterrent, Pappy had wrested control. His followers were convinced that only he had the knowledge which allowed them to return from the animal world to their everyday human forms.

Although he was unable to replace the magic water jar, the power of the Ya Ya had been sufficient to draw a handful of would-be sorcerers and sycophants to join his minions. In the hidden kiva behind Betatakin, Pappy was now the undisputed leader of the congregation, and they would, to a person, kill anyone who threatened the use of its power, for unlike the practitioners of the ceremony held in Chaco Canyon, these worshipers cared only for material gain or personal adulation.

Pappy had finally accepted the fact that without the magic water jar, there would be no use in trying to re-establish the Hopi claim to the lands now held by the Navaho. He had settled for the ego-stroking adulation of his followers, and the satisfaction of seeing the astounded expressions on the faces of those he chose to amuse or intimidate by some demonstration of his animal powers.

Pappy had entered the realm of the coyote so often that, at any given time, it was hard to know if he was functioning as an animal or a man. It had become more and more common for him to suddenly become aware that he was roaming the well-known ranch terrain on all fours; or trying to disguise an errant growl when something had displeased him. There were few men willing to stand their ground when Pappy chose to lock them in a penetrating stare from glinting, yellow eyes.

Around the ranch, it had been increasingly difficult for him to maintain the expected demeanor of the staid old cowboy. Of late, he really had little interest in the ranch, except for its acres of wilderness where he now spent the majority of his time. His tendency to wander the Earth in his animal form had grown to a compulsion.

They were having no luck finding Shaman and Rachel. Pappy called his acolytes together in the keyhole kiva.

"We will need the powers of our other selves," he pronounced.

While Pappy made ready to conduct the Ya Ya, Shaman led the little group of frightened survivors toward the new headwaters of the ever-increasing subterranean flow. This transfusion of pure water continued to seep into the myriad arteries and capillaries that fed the hidden geography of Mother Earth.

In the cavern where Shaman and Rachel had encountered the mutilated remains, the carrion, like necrotic cells that needed to be absorbed and eliminated by a healing body, were being carried away by the river. Shaman held Zoe closer to his side. He said a final prayer for the unfortunate souls. Some had probably been family sacrifices for the practicing witches. Others may simply have been in the wrong place at the wrong time.

Entering the cavern beneath Keet Seel, they could hear the rhythm of the Ya Ya above their heads. "Ya hi hi, huh huh," reverberated with a skin-prickling resonance.

The sipapu opening was tightly sealed. They were safe at the moment, but the water was steadily rising as the underground network of caves quickly filled. Shaman searched his mental library for a solution to this new quandary. One version of the Hopi legend of the great flood had Spider Woman seal the Chosen People into giant reeds in which the people were kept safe until the waters receded. *It's a great story, but not a reed in sight. If I remove the magic water jar from its new home, maybe the waters will stop rising. At least then we might be able to outwait them.*

Sham searched where he thought he had planted the jar, but the deepening waters had filled the well with the residue of the cave's belly, and he could not find the vessel's new resting place. The fresh infusion from the magic water jar had called forth the ancient sea, and the waters rose rapidly. Sham and the others were soon treading water several feet deep. Their heads were nearing the roof of the cavern, but the sipapu hole was still tightly closed.

The sounds above had lost their rhythm, disintegrating into a chorus of animal grunts, caws, and snarls. The Ya Ya dancers were shape-changing into their wild counterparts and had lost all resemblance to their once-human forms.

A small, harmless snake swam to within inches of Zoe's frightened eyes. It quickly submerged, and the waters began to churn. The little band was forced to clasp hands in a circle, trying to keep together and tread water at the same instance. From the center of the circle, the huge red-bellied snake shot above the water and through the crust of earth still barring their exit through the sipapu hole. The swimmers emerged with the rushing waters. They were surrounded by animals of every description, some of whom had not been seen in this area for many years.

Closest to the hole through which they had erupted was a large and fierce-looking coyote. Its sinister yellow eyes glared daggers at them, and it snarled its evil intent from slavering, snapping jaws. The great snake coiled itself around Zoe and, targeting the coyote, struck as quickly as lightning. Sinking its fangs deep into the coyote's back, the snake towered above them for a moment before releasing Zoe. The great reptile, with the howling coyote held firmly in its grip, slithered back through the sipapu hole and submerged beneath the rushing waters.

The waters continued to rise and soon poured over the edge of the ancient retaining wall into the canyon below, creating a crystal stream to meander along the canyon floor.

The animals scattered in all directions. The sipapu hole once again closed, leaving only a damp kiva floor and the astounded people congregated there.

EPILOGUE

The horses, along with the frightened Ya Ya dancers who had found themselves unable to return to their human forms, had abandoned Shaman's small party at the ruins.

The bedraggled band found shelter among the homes of their ancestors. One by one they drifted into dream-filled sleep.

Shaman was the first to reach that realm where sleep merges with reality. There, he sat with his mother on a large boulder. Below them, a small lake reflected the moonlight, taking on the appearance of quicksilver. The pair watched a variety of animals slowly approach and drink tentatively.

"You have done well, Shaman," said his mother. "I know it has been a difficult journey for you, but your work is not finished. Look at the wonderful new beginning that lies before us. The waters of the Earth are being transfused from their ancient forbearers. The animals have begun to return already.

"Without the power of the Ya Ya fostering greed and blinding them to the dismal future looming ahead, humankind might be returned to their rightful place in a nurturing universe. You must begin with the sun. Concentrate your efforts on developing ways to use the world's natural energy to provide for people's needs."

"What of the shape-changers?" asked Sham. "Will they ever return to human form?"

"I think not," replied his mother. "They will live now like their wild counterparts. Those two-hearts have caused a great deal of damage, and they must now help to replenish the animals' diminished numbers."

Zoe was having a vision of her own. The great red-bellied snake was gently swaying above her. She quietly addressed the now-familiar reptile.

You no longer frighten me," she said.

"That is good," replied the snake. "You have nothing to fear from me. You were willing to give your own life for others. As a protector of the Underworld, I have chosen you to help people understand the damage they have inflicted on their host. Now that you have experienced the world as it should be, you can help them make amends. You must study diligently. Lead your people to the means to heal the Earth, or its decaying corpse will consume them in its putrefaction."

"Alo will be your guide. You must develop your own ceremonial dance to call upon when the need arises. Remember what you have experienced. Use the lessons you have learned and incorporate them into your prayers. The snake faded from Zoe's dream. She woke briefly and felt a chill. She turned, and a warm mass of fur snuggled against her. Her faithful white dog had come to lie beside her. As she drifted back to slumber, Zoe was sure that her new protector would be with her always.

Clyde's dream whisked him away to the burning fires of the Underworld. The fierce coyote howled from the center of the flames. Clyde watched in fascination as the howling form shifted to that of Pappy Coyote and back again. The creature shifted once more to a shrieking Pappy, and Clyde heard the pitiful cries of a once-human being. "You still have time to save yourself," cried the nearly unrecognizable creature writhing before Clyde in the sulfurous flames.

"The power of the Ya Ya has helped to make you wealthy. Use that wealth and your knowledge of the law to turn the tide of greed. You still have time to reclaim the land. I followed the power of evil. Save yourself."

Pappy's last words were so distorted by the sounds emanating from his tortured body that Clyde could barely understand them.

In slumber, Rachel once again encountered her green-eyed benefactress.

"I feel that we are becoming old friends," said Rachel.

"We are much more than friends, dear Rachel. I am a part of you, and you will eventually return to me. Until that time, continue to nurture the children of the world with visions of what was, and can be again. It is not enough to share your love for nature with those close to you. You must find a way to share your memories with all those who have never been exposed to nature as it once was." She continued.

"Assist Zoe on her destined path to lead the people toward a higher plane. Zoe must build her future from her experiences in the Underworld. She will need your help to develop the rites of her dance."

Hyacinth slept the sleep of the faithful Hopi, certain that her spiritual guide would help her face tomorrow when it comes. For whatever the future held, Hyacinth knew she had always followed the Way and would be among the Creator's chosen.

She knew that from the abyss of oblivion, throughout the light of creation all that ever was and ever will be is already a part of us. As it winds its way along the path of infinity, our energy never really ceases to exist. It is only captured briefly by our earthly form, bringing us ever closer to a state of true spiritual enlightenment before rushing on to a giant wave, a towering volcano, a whispering wind, or perhaps a distant star. All is known and nothing is final as we continue our evolution.

THE END